Philip Threadneedle

he was at primary

Sadly, this is not the

to his ~~bestselling~~ cult classic novel *The Astronaut's Apprentice.*

You can reach Philip by sending an e-mail to philipthreadneedle@falconberger.co.uk.

wrote his first book when

it was fantastic

This is the sequel

CITY

OF

METEORS

BY PHILIP THREADNEEDLE

Falcon Berger

A Falcon Berger book
www.falconberger.co.uk
published by arrangement with the author

ISBN: 1467909963
EAN-13: 9781467909969

Set in fonts created by Ray Larabie
www.larabiefonts.com

10 9 8 7 6 5 4 3 2 1

This book is dedicated to

Noah and Tamsin, with love

CHAPTERS

SPLASHDOWN

THEY WERE RACING faster and faster over dark water.

Bradley had his face pressed up against a porthole. The sea reflected cold bright stars, like sequins under cellophane.

Suddenly, for a bit of fun, Grandpa dipped them right in the water, making it spray up on all sides.

"Ha ha!" he cried. "Look at us go!"

Before long, the porthole was swimming with water. Bradley felt as if they were on a ferry— to Calais, perhaps, or Cape Cod—or somewhere really exotic, like Hong Kong or even Penang.

But they weren't on a ferry. They were on a flying saucer, nearly four billion miles from planet Earth.

"We'll reach the coast shortly," said Grandpa. "Plus another ten minutes to the spaceport, and then we can land!"

He summoned a hologram of the planet and inspected it from every angle, like a snooker player lining up a shot. Then he measured their route between thumb and forefinger.

"Maybe twenty," he decided. "Hey—watch this!"

He grabbed a pair of levers and pulled them this way and that, like a skier shooting down a snowy alp. The spaceship dipped and gained speed as he pumped the long levers.

Grandpa was no normal grandpa. He was a bona fide alien. He'd returned to Earth some days before, and Bradley had jumped at the chance to join him in space.

Whoosh! went the spaceship—slicing through the waves a second time.

Now they had come to Grabelon, which was Grandpa's home planet. It circled the sun at a great distance, hidden from the eyes of Earth's astronomers. On the way there, they had picked up two new crew members. These were a one-eyed Plutonian girl, whose name was Headlice, and a floating furball called Waldo.

Headlice was at the next porthole, breathing on the glass and drawing love-hearts in the steam. Waldo was floating unhappily with his face to the ceiling. He was a strange kind of creature called *a star-pup.*

Somewhere between Mars and the Asteroid Belt, Bradley had learned all about the life cycle of the star-pups. It seemed to involve floating around looking worried, then singing a strange little song and bursting in a shower of babies.

"Bradley?" said Grandpa suddenly.

Bradley looked over his shoulder and saw that Grandpa was wriggling unhappily.

"I've got an itch," explained Grandpa—"but I can't let go of these darned levers—not even for a second! Can you do me a favour and *scratch the back of my neck for me?*"

Bradley didn't like the sound of that. The back of Grandpa's neck was covered in wrinkles and liver spots, with a hairy pink mole as well.

"What—scratch it? Really?"

He pulled a face. Even from the porthole, he could see the mole. It was like a little popped balloon.

"Do I have to?" he said unhappily.

"By the Great Red Spot!" cried Grandpa. "Yes!"

He wriggled his back, trying to neutralise the itch with his own shoulders.

"But be careful," he suddenly warned. "I'm *very* ticklish round there."

Bradley looked surprised and then shook his head.

"Headlice can do it," he said simply.

Grandpa cried out in frustration.

"*Either* of you!" he insisted. "Hurry!"

Bradley waited for Headlice to respond. When she didn't, he glared at her and went to the console. Before he could scratch Grandpa's neck, the old man gasped, ducked out of reach, and then burst out laughing at his own reaction.

"Ha ha! Sorry!" he said. "I'm *very* ticklish. Try again. I promise not to move."

Bradley rolled his eyes in annoyance and started to scratch Grandpa's neck for him. The old man screamed like a girl and fell to the floor, releasing one lever and yanking the other towards him.

Bradley went down after him. Grandpa's shoulders had risen in fright, trapping his finger against the horrible mole. It felt warm and hairy against his knuckle.

"Stop tickling!" shrieked Grandpa. "Stop tickling! I need to fly the ship!"

It was too late. The flying saucer smashed the dark waves and bounced across them, like a flat stone thrown at just the right angle.

Then it lost speed and ploughed heavily through the water, throwing up a curtain of spray.

At last, the spaceship came to a halt and bobbed lightly on the surface. Grandpa was in hysterics.

"Ha ha! Oh! Blimey!" he panted. "Blimmin' heck. I *am* sorry, Bradley. You wouldn't believe how ticklish I am."

Once he'd got his breath back, he sat up, reached behind his head, and gave his neck a quick scratch.

"Sweet Saturn's rings! That's *much* better," he said brightly.

He stood up and inspected the console. When he pulled the levers, nothing happened. Some of the lights were flashing. He fingered his moustache, twirling the wiry white hairs between thumb and forefinger.

Then he smiled.

"Aha!" he said. "*Now* I see what's wrong."

Bradley got to his feet and straightened his pyjamas.

"Why? What's up?"

Grandpa was looking through the periscope. As he did, water sloshed against the portholes.

"We're in the sea," he said at last.

Bradley pinched the bridge of his nose and counted to ten. The whole flying saucer was rocking like a yacht.

"You're a genius," he said.

Grandpa rolled his eyes.

"Stop being so sarcastic. You didn't let me finish. We're in the sea. The lift engine's wet. Short circuit—must have fried itself!"

He pressed a button, and the ship began to chug very slowly to the coast.

"We'll just have to float there," he said simply.

As they inched through the dark water, Bradley paced the cabin in a foul mood. He'd got used to zero gee, and now that he weighed something, he felt like a block of lead. To make matters worse, he couldn't even sit down, because the only chair onboard—a green sofa, with all the cushions crammed right into the corners—was mounted high on the cabin wall, and only accessible when they were floating around.

Waldo drifted overhead. He was permanently weightless, and therefore unaffected by being in space or out of it. Grandpa was leaning on the console, reading a newspaper with holograms on it.

After a while, Headlice left her porthole and went to give Bradley a playful punch. Her one blue eye was shining with excitement.

"This is brilliant!" she said unexpectedly.

He looked up at her and felt a pang of pity. With two eyes like a regular Earth girl, she would have been almost pretty.

"Brilliant?" he said. "Hardly. We'll be floating for hours before we reach land. Grandpa! Are we nearly there yet?"

She didn't look impressed.

"That's what little kids say," she reminded him.

"Oh, give over," he said bitterly. "I'm sure I'm older than *you*—so if I'm a little kid, then you're twice as bad yourself!"

Then he realised that he didn't know her age, and panicked that he might be younger after all.

"How old *are* you?" he asked quickly.

She smiled.

"Why—as old as my gums," she replied cryptically, "and a little bit older than my teeth!"

It took him a moment to work out what she meant. She'd dodged his question by saying something that would be true however old she was, because you're born with your gums and get your teeth a little later.

"I don't get it," called Grandpa from the console.

"Well I do," said Bradley. "It means—"

"Don't tell me!" snapped Grandpa. "If you got it, so can I. In fact, I just worked it out. Very funny Headlice. Very funny."

"Well done," said Bradley. "But seriously. How long before we reach the coast?"

Grandpa whirled on the spot with a wild look on his face.

"As long as my gums," he revealed with glee, "and a little bit longer than my teeth! Ha ha!"

Bradley sighed and straightened his pyjamas. He didn't have the heart to tell Grandpa that he hadn't got it after all. Then something occurred to him, and he punched the air with excitement.

"Hey—we're on Grabelon!" he cried—making Grandpa jump and drop his paper. "We've arrived! I can get changed into my space suit!"

The suit, which they'd bought in the Asteroid Belt, had been a bone of contention ever since. Bradley had wanted to wear it out of the store, but Grandpa had made him save it for Grabelon.

The old man smiled as he bent to retrieve his paper.

"Go on," he agreed at last. "You've been very patient. You can put it on."

Bradley jumped with excitement, ran to the storage cupboard, and slammed his hand on the bright panel. As the door whooshed open he ducked inside, making for the bag that contained his space suit.

"No one come in," he said sternly—closing the door behind him.

Five minutes later, the door whooshed open again. He paused in the doorway, pouting vainly at Grandpa and Headlice. Then he pulled a steely face and strode across the cabin, showing off his silver space suit. He had the mask slid back at a jaunty angle.

"Very handsome!" said Grandpa.

Headlice was more critical.

"You *do* look handsome," she said at last—"but the boots are a bit old-fashioned. Didn't they have any cowboy boots?"

Bradley was gutted.

"They did," he said. "But they sounded like high heels, so we said no. Was that wrong?"

"No! Hey—at the end of the day, it's your outfit. And from the ankles up, I love it."

He was heartbroken.

"What," he said dejectedly—"but only from the ankles?"

When she saw his reaction, she blushed bright red and rushed to console him.

"Oh—but it's no big deal," she assured him quickly. "I just like cowboy boots. And anyway—never mind that—what's the *sloppy stuff* that keeps hitting the windows?"

He forgot about his boots and frowned at her. After a while, he realised what she meant. She meant the water lapping at the portholes.

"It's just water," he told her. "We're in the sea."

She looked surprised.

"Water? Like a *glass* of water?"

Grandpa cleared his throat at the console.

"Remember that Headlice is from Pluto," he told Bradley. "No seas there! Just lots and lots of ice. I doubt she's ever seen more than a cup of the stuff."

She waved him to shush and ran to a porthole.

"Hang on," she said in horror. "All that wet stuff outside—is *water?*"

She covered her mouth.

"I'm going to have a panic attack," she said abruptly.

And without another word, she ran off to hide in the storage cupboard.

After she'd gone, something occurred to Bradley, so he turned to Grandpa with a question.

"We're further from the sun than Pluto is," he pointed out. "So how come there's an ocean here? It should be frozen solid. Surely?"

"Sub-surface heating!" said Grandpa.

"Grabelon is the most ancient of planets. Before it came here, it was drifting along through interstellar space. It can stay warm all by itself."

Bradley pulled a face. It sounded unlikely— but on the other hand, he'd challenged Grandpa before, and whenever he did he got egg on his face.

"Fine," he said. "Whatever. But where are we going to check in? You said the spaceport was twenty minutes from the coast."

Grandpa nodded.

"It is. There's been a change of plan. I know a submariners' town called *Deepover*. They don't like astronauts much, but if we're lucky, they might let us park with the subs."

He turned a dial very slowly to the right. As he did, the chugging sound got louder.

"Those lights on the coast are the harbour. If they let us park up, we can *ride a bubble* to Meteor City. That's my home."

Bradley went to a porthole and looked for the lights. When he found them, he saw that each was a different colour. They zigged and zagged down the dark coast, reminding him of fairy lights.

"Meteor City," he said out loud. "Sounds exciting!"

Grandpa grinned.

"It is," he assured him. "I guarantee you'll love it!"

MADMEN AND METEORS

BEFORE LONG, THEY were sailing through the beautiful towers of Deepover. These rose from the sea like shimmering coral, with round windows glowing on each level.

Bradley watched through the porthole. It was hard to tell where the sea ended and the town began. First they went past one tower, and then another, and then they chugged through a little group of them. Eventually there were more towers than open water, and Bradley guessed that they had arrived.

Just as he was looking for submarines, Headlice came out of the cupboard looking very pale, and said that she would look through a porthole if he went with her and held her hand. He stood unhappily beside her, trying to give her as few fingers as possible to hang on to.

"Why is it wriggling?" she asked him suddenly.

He looked at her.

"What—my hand?"

"No, you dumbo. The water."

He looked down through the porthole. In the dim light, he could see the ripples that raced on the dark surface.

"Oh, that. Well they're called *waves*. It's just the wind, blowing it around."

"Waves," she said softly. "Huh."

She pressed her nose to the porthole, watching them race along the surface. As she did, her breath made a silvery blob of steam on the glass.

"But why is it black?" she wondered. "Normal water is see-through."

"It's not black. It's just dark. And you can't see into it 'cos it's dirty."

She smiled and squeezed his hand.

"You're so clever," she told him. "But I still don't like it. It's way too much water."

24

And to emphasise her verdict, she drew a negative-looking cross in the steam on the porthole. Then she wiped her finger dry and walked away.

Eventually they sailed through a dark arch and down a long tunnel, emerging in a big wet chamber. Bradley ducked to peer up through the porthole. The walls curved to make a dripping dome, dotted with starry floodlights.

Suddenly, the whole console started to flash.

"That'll be the harbourmaster," said Grandpa.

He pressed a button. As he did, a brilliant hologram sprang out of nowhere.

"Oi!" barked the hologram.

Bradley jumped in surprise. The harbourmaster was a purple fishy creature with enormous eyes, lips like Cumberland sausage, and a glowing lure that dangled from his head. Because he was just a hologram, he filled the cabin with a strange blue light, and it was possible to see right through him.

"*You're* not submariners!" he said grumpily. "You're astronauts. Good grief. Is that a one-eyed pod-person? From Pluto?"

He was looking at Headlice. She smiled and waved.

"It is," said Grandpa. "Her name is Headlice."

"Well what's she doing in my hangar? What are *you* doing in my hangar?"

"In answer to your first question, she's on my crew," said Grandpa. "And in answer to your second, we ran into a spot of bother. We haven't got any lift. I hoped we could leave the ship here," he added hopefully, "and get a bubble to Meteor City."

The harbourmaster looked surprised, then delighted.

"No lift?"

He laughed, seeming to relish their bad luck.

"No lift! Well that's what you get," he crowed happily, "if you let a *Plutonian* on board. I wouldn't let her near my subs—that's for sure!"

Grandpa folded his arms.

"Headlice is a valued member of my crew," he replied coldly.

The harbourmaster just snorted and rolled his eyes.

"Fine. It's your crew and your funeral. But sure, why not. Leave the ship here."

He flicked the glowing lure out of his eyes.

"If you don't collect it within forty-eight hours," he warned Grandpa, "then we'll sell it for scrap. Good day!"

He vanished abruptly, leaving a stunned silence in the cabin.

"Scrap!" said Grandpa at last. "*I'll* show him scrap. Most of his subs are fifty years old! I wouldn't give you half a sausage for the lot of them!"

Bradley looked at Headlice. She was standing by the console, watching Waldo as he floated overhead.

"What did he mean about Headlice?" wondered Bradley.

"Oh—just a bit of *bad old-fashioned prejudice*," said Grandpa sadly. "I'm sorry you had to hear that, Headlice. If it's any consolation, they hate almost everyone in Deepover. Not just you."

Then he flicked a switch and pushed a lever, muttering angrily as he did.

"Scrap!" he said again. "Stupid fish of a man!"

They entered an empty alcove, lightly bumping the low platform. Grandpa thought for a minute and pulled a face.

"Bad news," he said at last.

Bradley went to a porthole. Outside, a rickety ladder ran down from the platform, vanishing into the water.

"Why?" he wondered.

Grandpa looked sheepish.

"Well basically," he said with some embarrassment—"we're going to have to *swim* out. Since the hatch is in the bottom of the ship, I can't think of an alternative."

Bradley was surprised.

"Really? That's literally the *only* way out?"

He looked around.

"There must be an emergency exit," he argued. "Surely."

Grandpa snorted.

"There *was* a spare lift engine," he said—"but I sold it to buy a pair of smart shoes. And there's an emergency exit of sorts, insofar as I keep a *stick of dynamite* in the cupboard—and when you've got one of those, all the world's an emergency exit! But to be honest, if it's just a case of getting wet, I'd rather swim out than blow a hole in anything."

He felt in his pocket and found a pair of nose plugs.

"Glad I've got these!" he said brightly. "So. Shall we get this show on the road, or what?"

Moments later, all three of them had left the ship and were shivering on the platform. Headlice looked especially traumatised. Grandpa had dragged her out by her ankle, and the poor girl had been sick in the water.

"Too much!" she said unhappily.

Bradley ignored her. He was trying to peer in through one of the portholes. They'd left Waldo on board, and since he ate pretty much anything—including furniture and metal—they'd left a tray of spare parts for him to nibble. Bradley could see the tray but he couldn't see Waldo.

"Will he be okay in there?" he wondered.

Grandpa ignored him. He was trying to get his nose plugs out. He'd done one nostril, but the other was stuck fast. After a while, he used his knuckle to seal the open nostril and pushed air into his nose. The plugs shot out and plopped into the water.

"What?" he wondered. "Oh—don't worry about Waldo. He'll be fine."

Before long an attendant came to the platform. He was a similar kind of creature to the harbourmaster, but he didn't have a lure, and his scales were orange with white stripes. He wore soggy blue overalls, waterproof wellies, and an enormous shiny badge with the word *Attendant* printed on it.

"You must be the astronauts," he said. "We have a saying in Deepover. *Only madmen and meteors come from space.* And you sure don't look like meteors! I suppose you want to ride

30

the bubble, do you?"

The bubble. That was the third time Bradley had heard about the bubble. He wondered what it was.

"We certainly do!" stammered Grandpa—smiling bravely as he dripped and shivered.

The attendant looked unimpressed.

"Then follow me," he said sternly. "And no clowning around! Especially not *you,*" he said pointedly to Headlice.

On the way out, they passed through a little room that blew hot air on them. The attendant tapped his foot and tutted while they stood around with their arms held out to dry.

Then he led them to a large chamber. This had a round platform right in the middle, and a circular cutaway high above their heads. Through it, Bradley could see some stars, with silvery clouds that raced across the sky.

"You're lucky," said the attendant. "There's normally a queue for this. On you go!"

The three of them mounted the platform. As they did, a bright sheen appeared around them.

It was a film of light, forming a bubble that enclosed them entirely.

"Meteor City," said Grandpa—speaking the words in a loud clear voice.

Something beeped and whirred.

"Destination not recognised," said a robotic voice behind them. *"Please try again."*

Grandpa licked his lips and gave it another shot.

"Meteor City," he insisted.

"Destination not recognised. Please try again."

Grandpa rolled his eyes.

"Blistering black holes! Meteor... *sitta-a-argh!"* he cried.

"Old Saturn Town," confirmed the voice. *"Commencing journey."*

Suddenly, all three of them lurched into the air. Grandpa kicked the bubble in frustration and called for help. In the end, the attendant had to go to a free-standing terminal and enter *Meteor City* manually.

The bubble detached itself from the platform and soared skyward, taking them out of the chamber and into the night.

"This is the bubble," explained Grandpa—spreading his limbs like a skydiver. "It's the quickest way to get around. You might want to put your arms and legs out," he added, "so you don't tip up when we change direction."

Bradley looked down and saw the attendant getting smaller and smaller. The fishy man waved them off and then slipped from sight, scratching his bottom as he walked away.

Then Bradley turned his attention to the bubble. He touched the inside of it. It felt strangely unreal, and resisted his touch like sun-warmed rubber.

"Is it airtight?" he wondered.

"No," said Grandpa. "Air can get in. You won't suffocate."

Then his face darkened.

"Don't trump though," he warned.

Bradley felt a rush of joy. It was great to be weightless again. Here and there, he could see other bright bubbles crossing the sky. As time went by, more and more joined them. Soon, they were leading a brilliant flock of bubbles that jostled and shone.

At last, they came to the most incredible city that Bradley had even seen. It was bejewelled with bright lights, and rose from the dark like a neon alp.

"Meteor City," said Grandpa with pride. "Home sweet home!"

Suddenly, three fireballs flared in the sky. The third was much larger than the others and exploded with a bright flash.

"Blimey! What was that?" wondered Bradley.

"Those are the meteors," explained Grandpa. "They come here because of a machine deep beneath the city. It's the oldest machine on Grabelon, and it's so old that no one knows how it works, or even where it is any more. They reckon the ancient Grabelonians caught the meteors and mined them for ore. Nowadays we let 'em burn up in the atmosphere. It's quite the tourist attraction!"

Bradley's heart leapt as more and more meteors streaked across the sky. Then he looked down and saw hundreds of other bright bubbles, all converging on the same incredible city.

"How do we get down?" he wondered.

He didn't have to wonder for long. Their bubble joined a queue and then sank into a dark funnel, entering a reef-like mass of the lumpy towers.

"Not long now," promised Grandpa.

It was only when they descended from the dark funnel that Bradley realised how high they were. The interior was brightly lit, and the sight of the far-off floor filled him with vertigo. Strange little figures dragged their luggage this way and that, making their way between hundreds of round platforms.

"Blimey!" he gasped.

It didn't take long for them to reach the ground. The bubble vanished with a faint pop, leaving them on one of the platforms. Some of the passers-by did a startled double-take when they saw Headlice, making Bradley feel annoyed and protective.

"Come along!" chirped Grandpa—leading them into the crowd. "We'll be home in a few minutes. I bet you're both ready for bed!"

Bradley yawned and nodded. Suddenly, he realised just how much he'd crammed into that one day. He'd flown through the rings of Saturn, fought a bunch of pirates, landed in the sea, and flown across the sky in a big glowing bubble. The mere thought of it all made him feel very sleepy.

Meanwhile, Grandpa marched them to another platform and cried out the name of his home address.

"North Star Apartments!" he bellowed. "Eighty-seven, Transneptunian Avenue!"

Instead of soaring high into the air, the bubble slipped out into the city, weaving this way and that through the lumpy towers. Bradley yawned and closed his eyes, taking a minute to rest them. They felt very heavy.

As they made their way through the strange city, a pleasant sensation washed over him.

"Bradley?" said Grandpa. "Are you awake?"

He was too sleepy to answer. After a while, he surprised himself by falling asleep—suspended in the bright bubble, unworried and weightless, dreaming of meteors.

TRANSNEPTUNIAN AVENUE

GRANDPA MUST HAVE carried him to North Star Apartments because he came to in a strange room.

He rubbed his eyes and looked around. He was still wearing his space suit, but his head had sunk into a giant white pillow, and a big weightless duvet lay across him. Floating overhead, humming as it hovered, was a globe of light that lit the room, throwing out hundreds and thousands of soft yellow rays.

It was a strange kind of bedroom. For starters, it was perfectly round, like the inside of a ping-pong ball. Stranger still was the tiny green man who waited by the bed. He'd been sitting on his backside, cleaning the dirt out from under his toenails with the corner of a playing card. When he saw that Bradley was awake, he sat up straight and put the playing card away.

"Hello!" he said brightly.

Bradley was too sleepy to do anything but stare. Then he yawned, lost interest, and went straight back to sleep, dreaming of comets over Camelot.

When he woke a second time, the little green man was still there. He was playing with the mask from Bradley's space suit, pushing it round the floor like a race car.

"Hello," said the stranger again. "Sleep well?"

Bradley rubbed his eyes and looked down at him.

"I did," he said. "Who are you?"

"I'm Benzo," replied the man. "I'm your alarm clock. I've been set for eight in the morning."

Bradley didn't know what to say. Benzo was only about a foot high. He was built like a Sumo wrestler, with folds of fat and flabby green arms. He had a funny little face with oversized lips, enormous wispy eyebrows, and delicate ears that were very nearly see-through.

"Well you can do it now if you like," said Bradley. "I'm up already."

Benzo looked delighted.

"Oh, really? All right then. Hang on."

He cleared his throat and took a deep, deep breath. His cheeks swelled and then darkened, and his whole body began to vibrate.

"*WA-A-A-A-A-A-A-A-A-A-A-A-A-A-A-A-A-A-A-A-A-A-A-A-A-A-A-H!*" he suddenly screamed. "Oh, man! Wake up! Wake up! It's eight o' clock!"

He buried his head in his hands and started to cry.

"Oh, man. Come on man," he sobbed. "It's eight o' clock. You gotta wake up. Wake up man."

Bradley tried his best to shush the little man.

"Hey! It's okay!" he told him. "I'm awake. You can stop it now."

Benzo wiped his eyes and looked up at him.

"Well do you want me to go on snooze? It means you can go back to sleep," he explained

40

helpfully, "and I'll wait five minutes before I do it again."

Bradley turned pale.

"Oh no," he said firmly. "Don't do that. Just switch yourself off completely. I'm up for good."

Benzo grinned and gave Bradley a big thumbs up.

"Then my work here is done!" he said happily. "Have a great day."

Bradley didn't want to hang around with Benzo, so he got up quickly, straightened his space suit, grabbed the mask off the floor, and went exploring.

Grandpa's rooms were very well-appointed. They were a maze of spherical white chambers joined by tubes, and some of the tubes were so narrow that Bradley had to crawl. The rooms themselves were filled with colourful clutter from all over the Solar System, including star charts, torpedoes, old space suits, and relics from the golden age of space flight. One little room had a toilet and sink, which Bradley used. It was far easier than going in zero gee had been.

Some of the larger rooms had level floors and were filled with beautiful antiques. In one, Bradley found a Chesterfield sofa with flashing blue lights instead of buttons. A weightless wooden ottoman bobbed beside it, rising and falling like a jellyfish.

In another, a coffee table supported a giant glass sculpture. As Bradley watched, the glass changed colour, becoming scarlet then purple then aquamarine.

Eventually, he found his way down to the living room, which was the largest of all the round chambers. Grandpa and Headlice were kneeling together in the centre of the floor, having a serious chat about something. They stopped and looked up when they heard him enter.

"Hello!" he said brightly.

He stepped carefully into the room. The carpet was soft and white like brand new snow, and just as deep. It had millions of weightless white fibres that stood perfectly upright. He trod on some and then lifted his foot, watching as they floated back into place.

"Don't let me interrupt," he added. "What were you talking about?"

Headlice looked guilty and played with the carpet.

"Oh—I can't even remember," she lied.

Grandpa looked surprised.

"You were saying you had a crush on Bradley," he reminded her.

She covered her mouth and blushed bright red.

"You idiot!" she said in horror. "You weren't meant to *tell* him!"

Bradley wasn't fazed. She'd only met one other boy in her life, and apparently, that first one had sported tentacles.

"You don't have a crush on me," he said firmly. "You just think you do. There's billions of boys in the universe and you've only seen two of us. How could you possibly know?"

She glared at him.

"Oh, just *drop it*," she said darkly.

He rolled his eyes.

"Okay, okay," he agreed. "Let's forget we ever had this conversation. How is everyone feeling?"

Neither answered, so he sat on the carpet before them.

"Well *I* slept like a log," he reported—running his hands through the clean white carpet. "I tell you what though—that's a funny alarm clock you've got up there!"

Grandpa frowned at him.

"Alarm clock?" he said suspiciously. "What do you mean, *alarm clock?*"

Bradley jerked a thumb at the ceiling.

"Oh, you know. Benzo."

Grandpa looked surprised and then furious.

"Benzo?" he spluttered—jumping to his feet. "Blistering black holes! Don't tell me *Benzo* is up there!"

Bradley was baffled.

"Well yeah," he said. "Why? What's wrong?

Isn't he the alarm clock?"

Grandpa purpled like a beetroot. He clearly couldn't believe what he was hearing.

"No he is *not* the alarm clock!" he thundered at last. "He's a weird little man from Mercury! I don't even know how he keeps getting in!"

Grandpa strode angrily from the room. Moments later he stormed back into it. In one hand, he was holding a round red clock with bells on. In the other, he had poor Benzo by his ankle.

"Come on!" barked Grandpa. "Out you go!"

The little man tried to wriggle free, but it was no good.

"Stop!" he cried. "I need to show you something! Something important!"

Grandpa just shook him under Bradley's nose.

"Does this *look* like an alarm clock?" he asked him. "Honestly! Does this *look* like a ruddy alarm clock?"

Then he showed him the clock with the bells on.

"*This* is an alarm clock," he reminded him

angrily. "Don't you have these on Earth?"

At last, he went to the front door, opened it, and tossed Benzo rudely into the street.

"And don't come back!" he shouted—slamming the door behind him.

Bradley and Headlice shared an awkward look. After a while, Grandpa turned from the door, walked across the room, and sat heavily on a club chair with metallic green piping.

"I'm sorry Bradley," he said at last. "I shouldn't have shouted. But that weird little man keeps appearing in my house, and I'm sick of it. If he shows up here again, I'm going to call the police."

He sighed deeply, took a moment to compose himself, then smiled and rallied.

"But never mind that!" he said brightly. "Let's decide what to do with our time here."

He went to a side room and came back with an enormous dark globe, which had the coastlines picked out in shining silver. He set it down on the carpet and span it slowly, showing them each of four continents. Parts of the globe were labelled *Peril* and others were labelled *Adventure* in glittering foil.

"We could hunt yogs on Rubble Beach," he began, with a faraway twinkle in his eyes. "Nothing tastes better than a yog you've caught yourself. Or we could look for treasure under Old Saturn Town. Or we could go to the zoo," he suggested, "and pet the star-dragons. Or we could just walk into town and grab some breakfast. What do you say?"

Before Bradley could answer, his stomach growled.

"That settles it," said Grandpa. "Breakfast it is!"

STARFISH STEW

THE WALK TO town was quite an eye-opener for Bradley. Grabelon's streets were a mix of mysterious avenues, raised bridges, and moving walkways that raced between the buildings. Along the way, there were booths selling bright green sausages, buskers of varying quality, and thunderous street preachers.

"It's coming!" cried one of them. He was holding up a tiny red book, like a football ref showing the red card. "The heat death of the universe—any day now! Only the Blue Shifter can save you! Pray for his magic shrinking fingers to catch us all!"

Bradley slowed to listen but Grandpa dragged him away.

"Don't make eye contact," he said firmly.

"Some of those guys are quite interesting, but that particular one just tries to sell you the book."

The denizens of Grabelon were weird and wonderful. A lot of them, like Grandpa, resembled silver-haired humans, betrayed only by a slight green tinge at the corners of their eyes. Others were thin and tall and covered in bristles, with arms like pipe cleaners. There were big hulking men with skin like stone, serene-looking yogis on magic carpets, and little green men riding giant caterpillars. The little green men looked just like Benzo, and Grandpa explained that the *Mercurials*—meaning people from Mercury—were very common in Meteor City, because their ancestors had helped to build the city's foundations.

It seemed to be rush hour. The roads of the city were paved with purple tarmac and had yellow taxis shooting down them.

"This is amazing!" said Bradley—jumping out of the way when he heard a car horn. "I've never seen anything like it!"

Headlice smiled and linked arms with him. As they made their way to the town centre, they passed a tiny dark building that caught Bradley's eye. It was barely bigger than a garden shed, but had two enormous bouncers guarding the front of it, and a neon sign that read *The Andromeda Club*. There weren't any windows, and the surface of the building was black and very smooth. A plush red carpet led through the open door and was swallowed by darkness.

He nudged Headlice and pointed it out.

"Look at that funny little clubhouse!" he told her.

Grandpa heard and glanced over.

"That's not the clubhouse," he explained. "That's just the lift. The club meets underground. It's not a nice place at all, but I believe it's very exclusive!"

Eventually, he took the children to a café and ordered three lots of something called *the Meteor City Special*. When it arrived, Bradley's heart sank. They each had been brought an enormous triangular dish, divided into four sections that contained different kinds of squishy space food.

He looked anxiously at Grandpa.

"I can't eat this," he said bluntly.

Grandpa rolled his eyes.

"Just try it," he insisted. "Trust me. It's the best food in the Solar System."

Bradley poked it unhappily with his fork. One of the sections was filled with a sort of snot-coloured broth. A skin had formed on the top of it, like you get on cold gravy. When he broke the surface, he found big orange peas, little red starfish, and unspeakable things that looked like ants.

"Go on," said Grandpa. "Try it."

Bradley inspected the rest of the plate. The other offerings were a silvery six ounce steak of some kind (which was blue in the middle instead of pink), boiled grasshoppers garnished with greens, and a kind of soft starchy veg with rainbow streaks running all the way through it.

"If you don't eat it," said Grandpa firmly, "then I'm sending you home. These Meteor

City Specials cost a bomb. They're highly regarded all over Grabelon. I'm not having you turn your nose up at our cuisine."

Bradley sighed and went for some veg.

"*And* the meat," insisted Grandpa. "That's the expensive bit."

"Do I have to?"

"Yes."

Bradley sliced off a tiny piece of the steak and added it to the mushy veg. Then he opened his mouth and gingerly put it onto his tongue.

His face lit up as he chewed and swallowed.

"Hey—it's really good!" he said in surprise.

He had another, much bigger mouthful, then felt brave enough to tackle one of the grasshoppers. They were sweet and salty like nuggets of bacon. Headlice, too, was wolfing down her own portion, pausing only to dab her mouth with a paper napkin.

Grandpa was delighted by their responses.

"Try the starfish stew!" he suggested.

Bradley looked down at it and wrinkled his nose. It didn't look appetising—but then, neither had the rest, and so far the meal had been delicious. He scooped up one of the starfish and dropped it in his mouth.

"Well?" pressed Grandpa.

He chewed slowly and thoughtfully. It came apart like braised beef, and had a strong gamey taste like wild boar sausage. The broth itself was rich and creamy like peppercorn sauce. After a while, he swallowed, grinned, and scooped up more of the delicious stew.

"This is actually really good," he admitted. "Really really *really* good!"

Grandpa nodded and reached for his fork.

"Thought so!" he said with satisfaction.

And he got stuck in himself.

Five minutes later, their plates were clean. Before they could leave the café to go exploring, Bradley felt a small finger prodding his knee.

It was Benzo.

"Hey! Is the big guy still cross?" the little man whispered.

Grandpa heard him and went bright red.

"By the ice-filled craters of Callisto," he swore quietly. "If that's Benzo—so help me—I'll kill him."

He wasn't exaggerating. The proprietor watched in alarm as he shoved the table aside to expose the trembling green dwarf. The knives and forks slid noisily from the table, and Bradley had to catch a triangular plate to stop it smashing at his feet.

"Well, well, well," began Grandpa, with a manic gleam in his eyes. "If it isn't my very best friend, Benzo. Hello chum. How've you been?"

He clicked his fingers at Headlice.

"Pass me the salt cellar," he told her. "I'll brain him with it!"

"Whoa. Hold on," said Benzo firmly. "Don't be so hasty with that salt. I've brought you something. Something to make everything cool again."

Grandpa looked at him in disbelief.

"Cool again? What do you mean, cool *again?*

When were we ever *cool?*"

Benzo looked shocked, then doubled over with mirth.

"Wowee!" he laughed. "Can you believe this guy? *He's* asking *me* when *we* were *cool.* Me and him. The original good time gang!"

He returned his attention to Grandpa.

"One word for you, captain. *Hyperion.* The burlesque bar in the Bahloo crater—remember that? How was *that* for cool?"

Grandpa made a surprised sound. It was halfway between a laugh and a sob but not quite either. Then he turned to Bradley.

"Never been to Hyperion in my life," he said flatly.

Benzo rolled his eyes.

"Okay. Look. We can row about it later. I want to show you something."

He pulled out a square of neatly folded paper. Against his better judgement, Grandpa took it, then prised it apart to see what it was.

At last, he snorted and spread it before him.

"A treasure map," he said. "Didn't expect

that. Where did you get it?"

Benzo smirked. By this point, he'd climbed onto a chair and was leaning on the table.

"What, me?—well—I get into places," he said cryptically.

"I'd noticed," muttered Grandpa—scanning the map.

Bradley sat up to get a good look at it—and as he did, a shiver of excitement raced up his spine. It was a funny looking treasure map. The paper was smooth and very nearly black. The detail was printed on it in silver. It had a decorative border of stars and planets, with rockets zigzagging between them. From some angles the print looked like graphite—but when Bradley moved his head, it caught the light and shone darkly.

He looked at Benzo and then back at Grandpa.

"Well it's not going to be *real*, is it?" he pointed out. "Alarm clock, treasure map— whatever next?"

"Don't be so sure," replied Grandpa. "I've seen a few old maps in my time. It certainly

56

looks the part. But with a map like this, there's only one way to make sure. Watch this."

He tapped three of the map's corners in quick succession. As he did, a star, a comet, and a crescent moon lit up at his touch.

"Thought so," he muttered. "Look—it's activating."

Then something very magical happened. The light spread from the corners to the rest of the map, making the design glow on the dark paper—slowly, like a fire catching. When the whole thing was shining brightly, the image rose clean off the page and arranged itself in three dimensions.

"Whoa! That's enough," said Benzo nervously.

He pulled the map towards him so he could fold it back up. As he did, the image warped strangely and then popped out of existence.

"Someone might be watching," he said darkly.

Grandpa raised an eyebrow in surprise. It looked like a wiry white caterpillar, Fosbury flopping high into the air.

"Someone?" he said. "Who? Why? Where did you get it, anyway?"

"I told you," said Benzo sourly. "I get into places."

Grandpa pinched the bridge of his nose, as if he had a migraine coming on.

"Right—but what *specific* places have you got into lately, Benzo?"

The green dwarf inspected his fingernails.

"All right," he said coolly. "The Mayor's house in Old Saturn Town. How's *that* for a place to get into?"

Grandpa looked impressed.

"You got the map there?"

"Well no," admitted Benzo. "No. That was just an example."

Grandpa grabbed his hair and groaned as if in pain.

"Sweet rings of Saturn!" he cried—lolling around in his chair and then emphatically headbutting the top of the table. "Just tell me where you got it!"

Benzo held up his hands to calm him.

"Okay, okay," he said. "It's mine. Honestly. Has been for ages. I bought it when I was young, but I lost it a long time ago. I only just managed to track it down."

He turned to Bradley.

"So how do you know my buddy?" he asked with a smile. "Is he a lunatic or what? Does he still have that stick of dynamite?"

"That's for emergencies," said Grandpa coldly. "It's not a toy. I keep it locked away in the storage cupboard."

Benzo laughed with delight and slapped the top of the table.

"What a lunatic!" he cried. "Am I right?"

He patted his pockets and rolled his eyes in annoyance.

"Look. Hold on to it for a second. I'm going to get some gum from across the street."

He pushed the map across the table, hopped down from his chair, and left the café.

Bradley watched him through the window.

As he did, he saw something very strange.

When Benzo reached the shop opposite, he

didn't enter. Instead, he flagged down a taxi and jumped inside.

"Grandpa?" began Bradley.

It was too late. The taxi scooted off into the city, leaving them with the mysterious treasure map.

NEVER TRUST A SAILOR

WHEN BRADLEY TOLD the others what had happened, they didn't know what to make of it.

"Well *that's* odd," said Grandpa—lightly fingering the folded map. "This must be worth something. Treasure or not, it's a legitimate antique. Why would he just leave it?"

Headlice held out her hand.

"Can I see it?" she asked shyly.

Grandpa looked down and pulled a face. Her fingers were still covered in sticky green traces of starfish stew.

"Well all right," he said unhappily. "But wipe your fingers first. Here, take this napkin."

She did as she was told, but the starfish stew had dried on her fingers and turned tacky. Instead of removing it, the paper napkin just stuck to it and tore.

"This napkin's useless!" she muttered. Her hands looked like they'd been tarred and feathered. "It's no good. Hey, Bradley. Open the map so I can look at it."

He obliged. As he carefully unfolded the creaky paper, a small white card fell out of it.

"What's that?" she wondered.

He picked it up.

"It's a message," he said. "Benzo must have tucked it in before he left."

"Well don't keep us waiting," said Grandpa. "Read it out!"

Bradley cleared his throat.

"It says, *Ethan,*" he began. "Wait—who's Ethan?"

Grandpa shrugged.

"Dunno," he replied. "He's called me Ethan before. I can only assume he thinks it's my name."

"Right," said Bradley. "Well anyway. It says, *Ethan. Old friend. Sorry to dump this on you, but I'm actually on the run from some very dangerous*

62

people. The map will be safer with you and your friends. I suppose that's me and Headlice, is it?"

Grandpa snorted.

"Remember this is Benzo," he cautioned. "He's delusional. For all *I* know, he thinks I'm friends with the Dixie Chicks! Carry on."

"Right. It says, *I need you to do me a favour. Find my people's treasure and return it to Mercury. You will find the rightful owners in the sun-blasted peaks of Caloris Montes, which are also known as the Mountains of Heat. You will be rewarded for this deed. Best wishes, Benzo. P.S.—whatever you do—don't let* The Andromeda Club *get hold of the treasure!*"

As Bradley read the postscript out loud, he remembered seeing the Andromeda Club in town.

"Grandpa," he asked—"what exactly *is* the Andromeda Club, anyway?"

"I don't really know," said Grandpa honestly. "There's a lot of crazy conspiracy theories about them. But as far as I can tell, it's just a bunch of super-rich rotters looking after themselves."

He ran his finger through the remains of his breakfast, then licked the tip of it with gusto.

"They've had their fingers in all kinds of pies," he resumed—wiping his own sticky finger on the side of his chair. "All sorts of shady deals. The latest scandal was something to do with blood diamonds from Venus. But they can afford the best lawyers, so they get off scot-free."

Bradley looked at the note.

"Well do you think any of this is true?" he asked.

Headlice's eye had narrowed with excitement.

"*I* think it's true," she said firmly. "The Mountains of Heat! They sound fantastic!"

"Well *those* are real," admitted Grandpa. "And about four hundred degrees at high noon—which lasts for days on Mercury—so I'm not sure we'll be able to visit! But this," he added—retrieving the map from Bradley—"this is real too. And if we have Benzo's blessing to hunt for the treasure, then I think that would be an excellent adventure."

Bradley wasn't sure—he didn't trust Benzo for a second—but when Grandpa unfolded and activated the map again, he forgot his fears. The three-dimensional image hovered over the table, bright and see-through like a glorious floating jelly.

After a while, the café door went *DING!* and a stranger walked in. He was one of the fish-creatures from Deepover, with rubbery lips and gleaming scales. He had black and gold stripes like an angelfish and was carrying a pile of little posters.

"Can I put one of these up?" he asked the proprietor.

When he just got a shrug in response, he went to the noticeboard, found a couple of spare pins, and attached one of his posters. Then he walked out with the rest of them, whistling as he went.

Bradley could see the poster from his seat. It said *Scrap for sale* and showed a grainy black-and-white photo of Grandpa's spaceship.

"Er—Grandpa?" he said nervously. "Have you seen the noticeboard?"

Grandpa looked over, spotted the poster, and turned bright purple.

"Blistering black holes!" he thundered. "I had forty-eight hours before they were going to sell it! Forty-eight hours!"

He shook his head in disgust.

"*Never* trust a sailor. That's what I always say, Bradley. Never trust a sailor!"

When the eavesdropping proprietor heard what had happened, he offered an explanation.

"They're submariners," he reminded Grandpa. "They won't use *regular* hours in a town like Deepover. They'll be on *Grabelonian nautical hours.*"

"Well how long is one of those?" wondered Grandpa.

"About three and a half minutes," said the proprietor. "Hey—is that girl a pod-person? From Pluto?"

Bradley rolled his eyes in annoyance.

"Yes, she's from Pluto," he said—butting in. "What's the problem?"

The proprietor held up his hands to pacify him.

"No problem," he assured him. "I just wondered. I'm not prejudiced."

"Well everyone else is," muttered Bradley.

Headlice poked his elbow.

"Don't make a scene," she said quietly.

The proprietor looked down at the two of them, then gave up and addressed his comments to Grandpa.

"You might want to go to Deepover," he said simply. "See if you can get your spaceship back!"

They got a bubble there. Instead of floating around with his limbs spread out, Grandpa sat scowling near the bottom, sulking with his arms folded.

"Never trust a sailor," he kept muttering.

"Never mind sailors," said Bradley. "Why does everyone keep looking at Headlice like she's got two heads or something?"

"Maybe it's because I've only got one eye," she pointed out.

"I'm not buying that," said Bradley. "This is Grabelon. I've seen men on flying carpets, green midgets, and giant caterpillars. One eye is neither here nor there."

"Prejudice," said Grandpa simply. "The pod-people of Pluto are rare, and they don't get around much. There are all kinds of stupid stories about them, and a few stupid people who still believe them."

"We're meant to be bad luck on a spaceship," said Headlice matter-of-factly. "Like it'll crash or something, just because there's a Plutonian on it."

"That's right," agreed Grandpa. "There's a rumour that their heads give off *brain waves* that play havoc with the instruments. Sorry Headlice. We're not *all* idiots here!"

When they got to Deepover, Grandpa jumped off the platform and stormed down a dark corridor. Bradley and Headlice struggled to keep up with him. When they reached a dead end, he stormed back the other way and tried a different route. It took them to an enormous swimming pool with boxes of wetsuits beside it.

"This place is worse than the methane mines of Makemake!" complained Grandpa. "Smellier, too! We'll never make it out alive!"

By the time they found the hangar where they'd left the spaceship, he was too tired to do any storming. He just sidled up to the little crowd who had gathered by his spaceship.

"Hello," he said in a weary voice. "Can I have my spaceship back?"

The harbourmaster was there with the attendant, who was wearing a wetsuit. A third tall figure was standing beside them. He had baby blue skin, navy blue hair, and a stylish orange suit with white lapels. Bradley recognised him at once. He was Wuztop Nash—the tailor from the Asteroid Belt, who had made his space suit some days previously.

"Oh—hello!" said Bradley in surprise.

When Wuztop saw him his eyes lit up.

"I remember you!" he said warmly. "How

nice to see you again!"

Bradley beamed and blushed.

"Why thank you!" he said.

But Wuztop's face hardened.

"I wasn't talking to *you*," he said coldly. "I was talking to that magnificent space suit. It outshines you so much I barely noticed you. For a moment, I thought it had come floating through the door of its own accord."

Grandpa, meanwhile, was pleading with the harbourmaster.

"Look—I'd never even *heard* of Grabelonian nautical time till today," he explained. "*Please* don't sell my spaceship!"

The harbourmaster scratched his head.

"Well we've sort of already sold it," he said awkwardly. "The gentleman from the Asteroid Belt bought it."

"That's right," said Wuztop brightly—cutting in on the conversation. "I've brought a new lift engine with me."

He pulled a glittering cube out of his suit jacket. It looked like a Rubik's Cube, only each of the squares was a different kind of gleaming metal. When he opened his fingers, it floated off his palm and hovered there, turning slowly.

"As soon as I've installed it, I'm going to fly that piece of junk back to the Asteroid Belt. Then I'm going to refurbish it and do house visits. Imagine that! Get fitted for a suit in the comfort of your own home!"

"But that's the problem," added the harbourmaster. "We *can't* install it. We can't even get on board. What *is* that monster you've got in there?"

Grandpa looked surprised.

"Monster?" he said. "There's no monster. Just a star-pup that young Bradley keeps as a pet."

Suddenly, a dreadful noise came out of the spaceship. It sounded like a blood-curdling battle cry. The attendant shivered unhappily in his wetsuit. Bradley suddenly noticed that his lips were covered in scratches, and he was even missing a scale or two.

"I managed to get my head through the

hatch," he explained. "Then I heard that awful sound, and this red *thing* came flying towards me. I barely made it out in one piece!"

Alarmed, Bradley ran to peer through a porthole. When he got there, he couldn't believe his eyes. Waldo—his adorable floating furball of a pet—was orbiting the hatch in the floor with a bloodthirsty look in his eyes. Every strand of his fur, which was normally white, had turned the colour of blood. His eyes were glowing bright red to match.

Bradley tapped lightly on the glass. Waldo saw him at the porthole and screamed with rage, flying face-first towards it—but he pulled back at the last second, seeming to recognise his master. He returned to the round hatch, glowering as he waited for another intruder.

"It's Waldo," said Bradley. "He's gone mental."

"Really? Well it must be a territorial response," said Grandpa. "I had no idea. I don't think people generally keep 'em as pets. Maybe that's why."

Then something occurred to him and he turned to Wuztop.

"So how do you plan to claim your purchase?" he said pointedly.

Wuztop shrugged.

"I'll call pest control," he said simply. "Let them go in with their special suits on and zap him."

"Can't," said Grandpa smugly. "Star-pups are a protected species. You might as well zap the harbourmaster here. You'd go straight to jail."

"Right," agreed Wuztop. "But it's no good to you either. I'm guessing you don't have a lift engine."

"Stalemate," noted the harbourmaster.

Headlice cleared her throat.

"Have you considered *sharing?*" she suggested.

Wuztop rolled his eyes in annoyance, but Grandpa was open to the idea.

"She's got a point," he said. "Give me the lift engine. I'll go on board, fit it, calm Waldo down—or lock him in the storage cupboard—and we can fly off together."

Then, with his back to the harbourmaster, he pulled out the map and showed Wuztop the corner of it. When the tailor saw the silver print on the dark paper, his eyes lit up.

"Do you know what this is?" said Grandpa quietly.

Wuztop nodded emphatically.

"With my ship and your lift engine, we can find it together," whispered Grandpa. "There's a reward. I'll give you a big enough cut to buy your own spaceship. Deal?"

Wuztop thought it over, then nodded and gave him the lift engine.

"Deal," he said. "But while you're fitting the lift engine, I want the children to wait on the platform. Otherwise, you could just fly off without me."

Grandpa grinned, then spat on his hand and held it out for Wuztop to shake. Wuztop just passed him a hanky and gestured for him to get on with it.

BRADLEY THE FUGITIVE

As soon as Grandpa popped his head through the hatch, Waldo relaxed. Satisfied that he no longer had to guard the ship, he faded from red to pink and then back to white, then floated off while Grandpa was looking for a towel.

Grandpa spent some time drying himself by the console, then tossed the towel away and got to work. Through the porthole, Bradley watched him fiddle with the new lift engine. He was twisting it this way and that, trying to make the colours on the sides match. At last, he opened a hatch on the console, pulled out the existing lift engine—which looked charred and misshapen—and popped the new one into the slot.

Almost straight away, the spaceship rose from

the surface, dripping big fat worms of dirty water. Grandpa made it hover over the platform, then threw a rope ladder down from the round hatch.

"Look what I found!" he said brightly.

Headlice went first. As Bradley followed, he saw the attendant give Wuztop a sharp nudge.

"Did you notice?" he whispered—loud enough for Bradley to hear. "One of the little ones is a Plutonian!"

"So?" replied Wuztop.

"Well you know what they say about Plutonians," said the attendant. "Bad luck! They give off *brain waves* that mess with the instruments!"

The tailor didn't look impressed.

"I know perfectly well what they say about Plutonians," he said coldly. "I also know what they say about Marilyn Monroe. They say she had twelve toes and was a size sixteen. Doesn't make it true. Step aside, you silly man."

He managed to get himself on board without any assistance. That achieved, he stood up

76

straight and scanned his surroundings.

"You ought to sort your ship out," he told Grandpa. "A rope ladder! Honestly! Is that how you *normally* get on board?"

Grandpa fished the ladder from the hatch. He'd tied one end of it to the bottom of the console and decided to dump the rest of it in the same spot.

"Nope!" he said brightly. "I literally just found it. We used to have an extending ladder, but it got ruined in a fight with some pirates."

Wuztop stared bleakly at Grandpa. He seemed to be wondering what he had let himself in for.

"You've got a rip in your space suit," he pointed out.

Grandpa fingered the torn edges.

"Happened when I was fighting the pirates," he said matter-of-factly. "You *do* like adventure, don't you?"

"Used to," said Wuztop. "Before I was a tailor, I was an explorer. But that was a long time ago. I'm in this for my cut of the treasure—*not* for fun."

* * *

Grandpa took them out of the hangar and high above the ocean. They went so high that the flat horizon turned into a curve. Before long, only stars could be seen at the portholes.

At last, at Bradley's request, they entered a giddy orbit, becoming weightless as they fell in circles round the dark planet. He closed his eyes, relaxing into zero gee. It was like slipping into a warm bath. Then Waldo came over and nuzzled his fingers. He stroked the star-pup's fur, relieved that his pet had gone back to normal.

"Does anyone mind if I put the news on?" asked Wuztop suddenly.

Bradley opened one eye. The tailor had removed his suit jacket and made himself comfy on the green sofa, which had its own field of gravity. When no one objected to his proposal, he pulled out a funny little gizmo with a dial, a red button, a round speaker, a telescopic lens, and two long antennae. He pressed the button, making an enormous fan-shaped hologram that filled the cabin.

"This just in!" the newsreader was saying. *"Reports of theft from the exclusive Andromeda Club, right at the heart of Meteor City!"*

Everyone looked up in surprise.

"Andromeda Club?" said Grandpa. "Meteor City? Turn it up!"

Wuztop obliged, and the newsreader continued.

"Our source confirmed that an antique treasure map has been stolen from the clubhouse. The chief suspect is one of the cleaners, Benzo Laruso, who hasn't been seen since the night of the theft."

Wuztop saw the look on Grandpa's face and raised an eyebrow.

"You didn't tell me that the map was *stolen*," he said coldly.

Grandpa turned bright red.

"I didn't know!" he said. "He told me it was his! I'll *kill* him!"

"Unconfirmed reports place Benzo at a local café this morning, where his accomplices took possession of the stolen map. We now go live to

Otto Rastaban, who is a founding member and lifetime president of the Andromeda Club."

The withered president appeared so suddenly that Bradley started with fright. He had a skeletal face with dark, sunken eyes, and a thin black tongue like liquorice.

"Yes, thank you. You're quite right. We've been working closely with the police, who tell us that the accomplices are already wanted on other charges."

"Charges?" muttered Grandpa. "Eh? What charges?"

"One of them goes by the alias Grandpa," continued the president. *"His real name is Ethan. He's a career criminal who escaped from jail eight weeks ago and met Benzo shortly after. As far as we can tell, they've been plotting the heist ever since."*

As the president spoke, he was replaced by an artist's impression of what Grandpa was imagined to look like. It showed someone who had the same hair and moustache as him, attached to what was basically a completely different face.

Grandpa was horrified.

"That is *not true!*" he gasped. "That is simply not true! Why would he say that?"

"Anyone who has seen Ethan should not, repeat not try to apprehend him," continued Otto Rastaban, *"as he is believed to be armed with a stick of dynamite."*

"For emergencies!" Grandpa protested. "It's for emergencies!"

"Ethan's right hand woman is a Plutonian called Headlice," continued the president. *"Aside from making spaceships crash, she's also thought to have masterminded a record-breaking missing trader fraud on her home planet of Pluto."*

Bradley looked at her, but she shook her head.

"I couldn't even tell you what that means," she said frankly. "Let alone do it."

"The third gang member is Ethan's grandson, Bradley. Before he left Earth, Bradley was embroiled in a cash-for-questions scandal, charged with drink-driving, and accused of expenses fraud. The Andromeda Club is offering a handsome reward for information that helps bring these

ne'er-do-wells to justice."

Bradley couldn't believe what he was hearing. He didn't have a clue what missing trader fraud or cash-for-questions meant, but he got the gist of the news story, and understood that they were being framed for all kinds of weird and wonderful crimes. He'd never been a fugitive before and didn't like it one bit.

Wuztop rolled up his shirt sleeves and carefully balanced his gizmo against the arm of the chair. Then he lunged across the cabin, sailing weightlessly towards the console. Grandpa saw what he was doing and tried to get there before him. They collided and began to wrestle.

"What are you doing?" cried Grandpa. "You'll make it crash!"

"I'm turning the ship around!" snapped Wuztop. "I don't want to be an accessory to your crime, and one reward's as good as another! I'll turn you in and buy a new spaceship with the bounty!"

As they fought, the newsreader continued to

read his bulletin.

"Thanks for that, Mr Rastaban. We're now getting reports of a fourth accomplice, who was put in charge of finding a lift engine for the getaway vehicle. His name is Wuztop Nash, and according to the Andromeda Club, he too is wanted on numerous charges."

The combatants froze.

"What?" wondered Wuztop. "*Me* wanted on charges? What charges?"

"According to our source, he kidnaps people and makes them work in his illegal sweatshop. In addition to these crimes, he has been cautioned for making prank calls, and was fined fifty pounds for animal cruelty when he sat on and tried to ride a dog that was far too small to support his weight."

Wuztop was mortified. He opened his mouth in protest, but before he could speak, Grandpa got him in a headlock.

"Turn us in? Turn us in, will you? *I'll* turn *you* in! I'll turn you inside out, you big blue dandy!"

He was so outraged by the short-lived mutiny

that Bradley thought he might actually have a heart attack. He floated over to defuse the situation.

"Calm down Grandpa," he said quickly. "It's not his fault. He trusted the newsreader. Even the newsreader prob'ly believes it. It's a stitch-up."

"He's right!" agreed Wuztop. "A complete stitch-up! I see that now. I really do."

Grandpa calmed down and released him.

"Well good job too," he said in a huff. "I tell you what though—they've shot themselves in the foot making up stories about us. If they'd just said that Benzo stole it and appealed for it to be returned, I would have flown straight back and handed it in. I'm no thief. But now I'm angry."

"You don't say!" muttered Wuztop sarcastically. "So what are you going to do?"

Grandpa produced the map, unfolded it carefully, and activated the three corners. Then he released it and gave it a light push. They all watched it float towards the centre of the cabin, with the three-dimensional image rising from the page.

"I'm going to keep it," said Grandpa. "Find the treasure, too. If there really *is* a reward, I'm going to claim it."

"And if there isn't?" pressed Bradley.

Grandpa's eyes shone as they followed the map.

"I'll sell the treasure," he said firmly. "And if there's no treasure, I'll sell the map. Either way, we'll all be rich. And when we are," he finished triumphantly, "we'll take out a *full page ad* in the Meteor City Herald, telling the Andromeda Club to eat their hearts out!"

THE ADVENTURERS' EMPORIUM

THAT SAID, GRANDPA went to the console and started yanking the levers this way and that. Bradley and Headlice fell against a wall as they turned very sharply.

"But first things first," said Grandpa. "We need supplies. Can't go on a treasure hunt without supplies!"

He turned to Bradley and winked.

"I know just the place," he assured him.

The next day, he revealed that he was taking them to a moon of Neptune called *Triton*. As they neared their destination, Neptune itself grew larger in the sky. First, it was a little grey speck. Then it was a gleaming drop of water. Eventually, it shone before them in all its glory, as bright and as blue as the Star of Bombay.

"One day, when we've got more time," promised Grandpa, "I'm going to take you on a trip to Neptune. We'll charter a ship and go whale-spotting. Won't *that* be something!"

He smiled, remembering the adventures of yesteryear. Then the console beeped, bringing him back to the present. He turned one of the dials and pressed all the buttons in order.

"But that's not why we're here," he said firmly. "We're here because Triton has a whole shopping centre, just for adventurers. It's the best place to visit before starting a treasure hunt. I've got a store card, so we can go nuts!"

When they got to Triton, he steered them into a fast orbit, shooting low across the surface of the moon. Through the porthole, Bradley could see glittering grey plains and crisp dark craters. He even saw icy volcanoes, spewing chilled water instead of lava.

"Any second now," Grandpa promised. "Ah— here we are!"

There was a round dark crater ahead of

them—more like a deep pit than a crater—with something long and red glowing on the far side of it. Whatever it was, it wound through the ice like a river of fire. As they overshot the crater, Bradley realised that the red light was in fact a giant neon sign, lying flat on its back in the frosty grey plain. It simply said, ENTRANCE.

"Hold on!" cried Grandpa.

Only then did Bradley realise that the crater was a hole in the moon's surface. He grabbed a rail as they plunged wildly like a ghost train, entered a steep dive, and vanished down the dark tunnel.

He had to hold on with all his might. He looked over his shoulder and saw that Headlice and Wuztop were pressed flat against the back of the cabin. Waldo was there too—squashed against the wall like a thrown snowball.

At last, just as Bradley was about to lose his grip and go flying up to join them, they levelled out and slowed down.

"Sorry," said Grandpa from the controls. "Didn't mean to speed up like that."

Bradley had a look through one of the portholes. They had arrived in an enormous glittering chamber. It was easily five hundred feet high and lit from below with waving searchlights. The space contained hundreds of shops that had been stacked up on top of one another.

He pressed his face to the glass. They weren't organised properly, like shops in a shopping mall. They were heaped up like piles of old boxes, with zigzagging stairs and wonky walkways. The shops themselves had bright windows, chaotic displays, and neon signs that flashed and fizzed like fireworks.

"This is the Adventurers' Emporium," explained Grandpa—steering the ship to a floodlit parking lot. "I'm going to give you children a shopping list. The four of us together might be too obvious—now that we're *fugitives.*"

And he smirked to himself at the console, clearly enjoying the thought of himself as a fugitive.

The parking lot was very full. Their spaceship jostled the others, setting them off like boats bumping on a lake. Once they finally stopped moving, Grandpa went to the storage cupboard.

"Wuztop and I will remain here," he announced over his shoulder—making a racket as he rummaged around—"and make a start on deciphering the map. Off you go!"

Bradley and Headlice looked at one another.

"We haven't got the list yet," complained Bradley. "*Or* money."

As he spoke, Grandpa emerged with a bottle of whisky, two glasses, and a pair of stripy deck chairs.

"What?—oh—good point," he agreed. "Hang on."

He found a pen and paper, jotted down a few things, and pressed the list and pen into Headlice's hand. Then he presented Bradley very solemnly with his store card.

"All the shops here accept it," he said. "Just put everything on the card and I'll sort it out later."

That achieved, he gestured for Wuztop to unfold the chairs, unscrewed the top of the bottle, and waved for the children to make themselves scarce.

Bradley dropped through the hatch and onto the tarmac. Headlice did the same and the hatch *whooshed* shut.

"Come on," said Bradley—waving for her to follow. "I don't like it here. Let's get out into the open."

She ignored him and stood beneath the hatch, gawping up and all around. Hundreds of spaceships were jostling above them, throbbing with strange energy. Even though they floated in the air, it was obvious that they were very heavy. They bobbed slowly like bricks on elastic.

Bradley remembered the first time he had looked up to see a spaceship hovering over him. It was even worse knowing they were held up by tiny lift engines, which could fail. Standing under one was like standing under an enormous chandelier, with nothing but the thinnest, tautest of cords to stop it falling.

Then he spotted a small sleek spaceship that stuck out like a sore thumb, and made him uncomfortable for a reason that he couldn't quite put his finger on. It was a metallic purple colour, with two large portholes and six smaller ones on the underside. These were tinted so you couldn't see up into the cabin, and reminded him so vividly of a spider's eyes that they made his skin crawl.

"Come on," he told Headlice. "I want to get out of here."

She looked surprised, then shrugged and followed him as he power-walked away. He kept his head down, scowling at the ground until they were clear of the parking lot.

Before long, the higgledy-piggledy shops loomed all around them.

"Right. What's on the list?" wondered Bradley.

She consulted the piece of paper. Then she smiled and let him see.

"Lots of stuff!" she told him. "It'll take *hours* to get through it all."

Bradley read the list. It said, *Peanuts and/or crisps. Magazines. Torches. Self-inflating four man dinghy. Life jackets. First aid stuff. Laser swords. Distress flares. Sun cream. Chocolate peanuts. Cereal bars. A laser rifle. Bag of mints. Ropes. Four man tent.*

"It's not *that* much," he pointed out. "And I'm not even sure we need half of these things. We certainly don't need chocolate peanuts *and* normal peanuts."

He looked up. The brightly-lit shops towered above them like a stack of televisions, each showing something different.

"We better get started," he said with a sigh.

They traipsed up and down the wonky stairways, inspecting the different shops. One had the most incredible display in the window. Behind the glass, a blizzard of real snow fell from the ceiling, almost burying a silver tent. The spidery flakes melted as they stuck to the canvas, like cold white pearls becoming clear bright diamonds.

The tent looked big enough for four.

"That'll do," said Bradley. "Cross the tent off!"

Before long, they had bags and bags of stuff. Bradley carried the lion's share of them, trying to make it look easy. After a while, Headlice noticed him struggling and relieved him of the heaviest bags, which she ended up dropping everywhere.

"Let's take a break," she suggested.

They got some enormous fizzy drinks from the floating food court and stood around drinking them. Bradley sipped his very gingerly. The drinks came in enormous plastic beakers, with crushed ice, curly straws, and paper umbrellas the size of saucers.

"So what's Earth like?" asked Headlice suddenly.

"What—*planet* Earth?"

"No!" she said sarcastically. "I mean soil. What's *soil* like, Bradley? Of *course* planet Earth, you doofus."

He shrugged and let his eyes wander. One of the shops opposite had an underwater display, with mannequins wearing deep sea diving suits.

"It's all right," he said at last. He was surprised to see real fish darting back and forth across the display. "I mean it's not as good as space. But it's okay."

"And what about your family?"

"They're a bit weird," he admitted. "Grandma's crazy and Mum died when I was a baby. Dad keeps her in the loft. She's frozen in some kind of capsule."

"Oh really? Well on Pluto," she said helpfully, "we *bury* people after they die."

He rolled his eyes.

"Well so do we," he said irritably. "Obviously. But I think he wants Grandpa to bring her back to life. Using *alien technology* or something. I keep meaning to bring it up with him, but I'm worried he won't be able to do it."

He fell silent. He didn't have anything more to say on the subject of family. He tried to come up with something to ask her in return, but couldn't think of anything.

He scanned the crowd for inspiration. Very quickly, his eyes fell on a strange tall figure who was standing on the far side of the food court. The figure seemed to be looking right at him. His face was dark purple, like an aubergine, and very nearly as shiny. He had two big eyes like polished jet, and six smaller ones that made him look like a giant spider.

He held Bradley's gaze for five, ten, fifteen seconds. At last, he looked away. Before Bradley could point him out to Headlice, she got bored of the silence and ploughed on without him.

"By the way," she added—"I wanted to thank you. For trying to stick up for me the other day."

He forgot the strange man and looked at her in alarm.

"Stick up for you?" he said. "Why? When did I try to stick up for you?"

She slurped her drink shyly.

"When the man in the café asked if I was from

Pluto. I don't think he was being rude, but I do appreciate you telling him off."

Bradley snorted.

"Don't worry about that," he said dismissively. "You're a nice enough person. You don't deserve all the grief you've been getting."

He finished the last of his drink, took the beakers to the bin, and then picked up as many of the bags as he could carry. Headlice took the rest and they went off to finish their shopping.

As they did, Bradley realised that the stranger was walking the same way as them, about twenty yards behind.

"Don't look now," he said to Headlice, "but I think we're being followed."

Her shoulders tensed in alarm.

"Right," she said quietly. "But the thing is, now you've said that, I prob'ly *am* going to look."

He pulled a face, wrestling with the temptation to do exactly that. Then he gave up and looked.

"Well do it now," he told her. "He's trying to act like he isn't paying attention."

She joined him in staring. The stranger was standing in a shop doorway, stroking his chin and pretending to study the opening times with all eight of his eyes. He read and re-read the times for each day, then leaned in to scan the bit about Bank Holidays.

"All right," said Bradley quickly. "Stop looking now. He can't read that sign forever."

As they hurried away, Bradley glanced at a shiny shop window. Among the reflections, he could see the eight-eyed stranger making to follow. Then he realised, to his horror, that a second figure was standing *inside the shop window,* mingling with the mannequins and watching through the glass. He too had eight eyes and a shiny purple face. As Bradley stared, the stranger withdrew and vanished into the darkness of the shop.

"I've got a bad feeling about this," he told Headlice. "Quick—down those steps. We need to get back to the ship."

They mounted the stairs at normal speed, as if they had all the time in the world. The second they were out of sight, they started running down them. When they reached the bottom, Headlice made in the direction of the parking lot, but Bradley dropped his bags and grabbed her sleeve to stop her.

"It's too exposed," he said. "Come on. We'll go round the back of the shops, if we can."

Struggling with the bags, they squeezed between two of the buildings and were soon lost in a maze of alleys. Some were so narrow that they had to go single file. Others were wider and had shady-looking people hanging around them.

Then they stumbled on a secret market, hidden by the backs of the crooked buildings, where goods were sold out of open crates. In the centre of the market, a wily entrepreneur with one round eye and countless waving tentacles had set up stall on an upturned box. He was running a crooked game of Three Card Monte, rigging the cards so he won every time.

Bradley soon lost all sense of direction.

"I don't know where we're going," he said wearily.

"Don't worry!" said Headlice brightly. She grabbed his wrist and led him firmly from the market, down one alley and through several more. "I know exactly where we're going. My mental compass is impeccable!"

Even as she spoke, Bradley realised he could hear the gentle hum of spaceships hovering. His heart leapt as she pulled him out of the alley and into the parking lot.

It took him a moment to spy their own spaceship. Then he looked back in the direction of the shops. Three figures were having a heated discussion at the bottom of the stairs. Bradley recognised the one who had followed them and the one from the shop window. The third looked exactly like the first two, except he was half a head taller and wore five black eyepatches. These criss-crossed his purple face, covering all but three of his beady eyes.

"Let's get on the ship," said Bradley.

They stood below it and shouted up to Grandpa. After a while, the ship lowered unsteadily and the hatch *whooshed* open.

"What?" said Grandpa irritably. He sounded a bit drunk.

"Quick—take the bags," said Bradley. He picked up the first and held it high above his head. "I think we're being followed."

Grandpa obliged and then threw the rope ladder down. Headlice went first. Before Bradley could follow, he realised to his horror that the three strangers had spotted them, and were now walking purposefully towards the parking lot.

"Hurry!" he told her.

"All right," she snapped. "I've got my foot stuck. I'm going as fast as I can."

The minute she freed herself, Bradley climbed up through the hatch and pulled the ladder in after him.

GRANDPA GETS A HEADACHE

BRADLEY'S HEART SANK when he looked around the cabin.

Wuztop was slumped in one of the deckchairs, reading a pile of typewritten pages. He had one eye shut so he could focus. There wasn't much whisky left in his glass, and neither was there much left in the bottle. The treasure map, which they were supposed to be deciphering, was folded up on the console.

"Are you drunk?" asked Bradley in annoyance—briefly forgetting their pursuers as he dumped the rope ladder by the console. "I thought you were meant to be looking at the map?"

Even Waldo seemed to have tried a bit of whisky. He was floating upside down with a puzzled look on his face, as if he couldn't quite work out what was different.

"We *did* look at the map," said Grandpa. "We worked it all out. Then we had a few more drinks and now Wuztop is reading my novel."

Bradley shook his head in disbelief.

"Your *novel?* Grandpa—honestly—we've got to leave," he said. "Right now. Three men were looking for us in the Emporium, and now they're coming to the parking lot."

Grandpa rolled his eyes in boredom.

"Oh, *blah blah blah*," he said. "Well *I* can't fly the ship. I've been drinking. Come on Bradley. You do it. I'll tell you how."

He pushed him towards the console.

"Turn the roundest of the dials," he began unhelpfully, "in the direction of *itself*."

Bradley covered his eyes and groaned softly. Before he could reply, a gruff voice called up from below.

"All right," said the voice sharply. "Enough nonsense. There's three of us here and we're armed. We're working for the Andromeda Club, so throw the map down before we get nasty!"

Grandpa pulled an exasperated face.

"Oh, *blah blah blah*," he said again. "All right. I'll get your map. Wait there."

He hiccupped, went to the storage cupboard, and emerged with his stick of dynamite. It was bright red and had a long black fuse, which sputtered and spat.

"Here's your map!" he jeered—dropping it down the hatch.

"Run!" cried the voice below.

Moments later, an explosion rocked the whole ship, making Wuztop's deckchair collapse under him.

"I'm all right!" he called drunkenly.

Grandpa picked himself up off the floor, then went to the console and waved for Headlice to join them.

"All right kids," he told them. "We don't have much time, and I'm starting to get a headache. Levers. Pull the main ones in opposite directions, then press all the buttons in time."

Bradley cried out in frustration.

"Grandpa! That's *not* helpful!" he told him.

"Well look," said Grandpa—and he showed him exactly what levers to pull, and which directions to pull them in, and got Headlice drumming the buttons.

They started to move. Bradley's head was spinning. Under Grandpa's direction, and with Headlice's help, he was *actually flying the spaceship.* Grandpa pointed out this and that thing on the display, making sure he pulled the right levers at just the right moments.

Wuztop staggered to one of the rear portholes.

"They're following on foot," he said. "Three of them with guns. Let's get out of here, before they start shooting."

Bradley ignored him. With every passing second, they moved faster and faster towards the exit.

"Ha ha!" he cried. "I'm doing it! I'm flying the spaceship!"

At last, as the first gunshots sounded below, they rose up through the surface and into the sky, over the glittering peaks of ice volcanoes.

* * *

Once they were sufficiently far from Neptune's icy moon, Grandpa directed Bradley to plot a course.

"We need to find a *dwarf planet*," he explained. "It orbits the sun at a great distance. The orbit is described by the map, so it should be easy to calculate its current position."

That achieved, he looked around for something to do. Wuztop had nodded off by then and was floating around with his mouth open, so Grandpa had to sit on the sofa with no one to talk to. After a while he became depressed. Then he burped and fell asleep.

When the adults came to a few hours later, they were both sick from drinking so much whisky.

"I'm never doing that again," muttered Wuztop—rubbing his temples. "I forgot about hangovers!"

"Agreed," said Grandpa gravely.

He looked a lot older and paler than normal, and even his moustache seemed to be sagging under its own weight.

"I do apologise," he told Bradley and Headlice. "It was very stupid of us to sit around drinking whisky like that."

"Well it made you act ridiculous," said Bradley bluntly. "You'd think a man of your age would know better! Don't you want to know who was chasing us?"

"Go on," said Grandpa wearily. "Tell us all about it."

"They had purple faces and eight eyes," said Bradley. "One had a whole load of eyepatches."

Grandpa went as white as a sheet.

"Those are arachnids," he said quietly. "Notorious assassins. If the Andromeda Club hired a gang of them to hunt us down, then to be frank, we're in trouble. I wonder how they knew we'd be there?"

"Because it's the best place to visit before starting a treasure hunt," replied Bradley— quoting Grandpa's exact words from earlier. "Where else would we be?"

Wuztop groaned. He was pressing an ice pack

to one of his eyes.

"Did I dream this, or did one of the arachnids have five patches?" he wondered bleakly. "That's the Black Baron! He's the worst of the lot!"

Headlice was floating high overhead, trying to get Waldo to submit to being stroked.

"Funny name for a hired killer," she chirped— just as he dodged out of reach. "I thought barons didn't have to work?"

Wuztop shrugged.

"Maybe he enjoys it," he said darkly.

Suddenly, Bradley lost patience with the whole fiasco.

"We should hand the map over," he told them bluntly. "It's not even ours, and it's certainly not worth getting in trouble over. We should have told that idiot Benzo to keep it."

But Grandpa's eyes lit up at the mention of the map.

"You say that," he told him—"but remember, we've cracked it now. Look."

He got the map from the console, unfolded it,

and activated it with three deft touches. As he spoke, he made gestures with his hands, causing the three-dimensional image to spin like a globe. When it stopped, it showed a range of red-hot mountains under the sun.

"Caloris Montes," said Grandpa. "The Mountains of Heat. The treasure was owned by the king of these mountains. He lives in an air-conditioned castle on the tallest summit. Now according to the map, the treasure was hidden long ago, and you can only get to it via a *portal*. The portal is like a kind of teleporter. It transports you across space and time in an instant, to the treasure chamber itself. But the portal only goes one way—and it's buried in an old mine far from the sun. That's where we're going now. To find the portal!"

"If it only goes one way, then how do you get back?" wondered Headlice.

Wuztop decided to chip in.

"There's a second portal," he said—putting his ice pack aside. "An exit. It whisks you straight from the chamber to the king's throne room."

Bradley was losing patience with the idea of treasure, but he couldn't be bothered arguing. He just floated to the roof of the cabin and helped Headlice to corner Waldo. Before long, they had the poor creature trapped between them, and were running their hands through his cool white fur.

The next day, as they made their way further and further from the shrinking sun, Grandpa got a phrase book out and tried to translate the rest of the map.

"The treasure is a goblet full of gems," he said at last. "I *think* it's gems. The gemstones of Pluto. What are the gemstones of Pluto?"

Headlice shrugged.

"Never heard of them," she said. "And I'm *from* there!"

"Well they sound lush!" said Grandpa. "They're rarer than diamonds—clearer and brighter than stars, with glittering facets that catch the light. And the goblet refills itself when you pour out the gems. The king used to hand out cups of them on feast days, but it didn't matter, 'cos the goblet just filled right up again."

"Imagine that," said Wuztop wistfully. "A whole cup of diamonds!"

Bradley wasn't convinced.

"I think diamonds would be a lot cheaper," he pointed out, "if there were magical goblets literally overflowing with them."

"Well of course," agreed Grandpa. "It's just a fable. An exaggeration. It's probably a diamond-studded chalice or something."

On they went into outer space, getting further and further from the known planets. After a while, Grandpa announced that they were even further out than Grabelon. There were billions of miles between them and the sun, and outside, he warned, it would be cold enough to freeze the blood of a comet.

"Just think," he said in an excited whisper. "Any dwarf planets here will take centuries to orbit the sun. Just imagine them, winding their way slowly through the darkness. Just imagine how *cold* they'll be! Why—we must be about *ten billion miles away* from our little white sun."

He looked through a porthole and shivered.

"So I should prob'ly get the electric heater out," he finished gravely.

The electric heater was about the size of a toaster and had a little fan in it. It plugged into the wall and made a soft roaring sound as it filled the cabin with warm air. Soon, they were all nice and toasty in the cabin, even though they were billions of miles from the sun.

Then they had what Grandpa called their *tea*—meaning the evening meal, rather than the hot drink—which came in squishy foil bags, like fat tubes of toothpaste.

As they slurped up the soft food, they got to know Wuztop a bit better. He recovered from his hangover and began to tell them stories about his former life as an explorer. His blue face purpled with pride as he recounted tales of derring-do in the icy craters of Callisto, with Jupiter—which he called *Old Jove*—filling the sky like an angry red balloon.

"I travelled for a while with a man from Pluto," he told Headlice. "Fellow by the name of *Headfungus*. Had only one eye, but was very brave. I flew on the same ship as him a hundred times and there was never a problem. Not one hiccup. So I never believed all those tall tales," he finished nobly, "about your brains giving out interference and making things crash."

Once Wuztop was done with his story, Grandpa rose to the challenge. He told the tale of how he'd once been cornered by sand-sharks on Mars. He'd fought them off with a mammoth's tusk in one hand, and a sword forged from a meteor in the other.

"It inspired a scene in my novel," he said proudly. "It's very exciting. Maybe I'll read it to you later."

Luckily, he never got round to it. Instead, they took turns to wash in the little wash room at the back of the storage cupboard. Bradley chased a weightless globe of water around, breaking it up in his fingers to clean his face and hands and armpits. When he was done, he pulled the plug out of the sink. The shimmering orbs were sucked into the plughole and blown into space.

Suddenly—unexpectedly—he felt a little pang of homesickness. He yearned to be brushing his teeth over his own sink, and getting ready to climb into a normal bed. He missed the feeling of Earth's gravity pulling him down into a soft mattress.

He returned to the cabin and got comfy on the sofa. Headlice was already fast asleep.

"Night night," he said—getting a cushion to use for a pillow. "See you tomorrow."

Before long, lulled into silence by the warmth from the heater, they each joined Headlice in sleep, leaving only the sound of hot rushing air to fill the cabin.

THE MAGNIFICENT SUN-SLUG

THE NEXT MORNING, they were roused by the sound of robotic chatter. Captain Nosegay had come alive on his pedestal.

Bradley sat up on the sofa and rubbed his eyes. He'd forgotten about Captain Nosegay. The rarely-seen Captain was nothing more than a disembodied brain with a giant nose attached to it. He lived in a glass dome by the console and helped Grandpa to navigate from time to time.

"*Attention!*" he told them. "*Unknown dwarf planet dead ahead!*"

His voice came out of the console speakers. As he spoke, his enormous nostrils quivered and flared.

"*Diameter, three thousand kilometres!*" he

reported. *"Composition, mostly rock and ice! Atmosphere, breathable!"*

Bradley wasn't convinced.

"Atmosphere? Is he *sure* there's an atmosphere? This far from the sun," he pointed out, "I would have thought even *air* would be frozen solid."

"Well it's always a treat to hear your views on the subject of space," said Grandpa sarcastically, "since you are of course an expert. But I think I'm going to trust the Captain on this one. It *is* odd, but there are plenty of anomalies in space, and maybe we'll solve the riddle later."

Bradley could see it through the porthole. It was like a snowball made of compacted blue slush.

"So the treasure is there, is it?" he wondered.

Grandpa shook his head. He'd gone to the console and was cracking his knuckles, ready to take command of the ship.

"The *portal* is there," he reminded him. "The treasure itself could be literally anywhere. But the portal will take us straight to it. And according to the map, the portal is at the deepest point of an abandoned mine not far from here. Once we find the portal, we can fetch the gemstones of Pluto, return them to Mercury, and claim our reward!"

He pulled the levers, making them whirl around the planet in ever-shrinking circles. The dark mass grew larger and larger until it took up half the porthole, making a curved horizon that got flatter and flatter.

Then they began to slow down.

"Nearly there," promised Grandpa.

Before long, they weren't weightless any more. The surface of the planet sparkled like blue granite in all directions.

Then Bradley saw something ahead of them. In the side of a jagged mountain, leading down into the planet's interior, was a dark round tunnel. The whole mountain sparkled like sugar, making the tunnel itself seem even darker.

"Bingo," said Grandpa. "That must be the entrance to the mine. Not sure we'll fit the spaceship in, so we'll have to go in by foot.

Captain! How cold is it out there?"

"*About twenty degrees below zero!*" replied the Captain.

Grandpa looked horrified and rubbed his arms.

"Crikey!" he muttered. "Twenty below!"

Bradley couldn't believe what he was hearing.

"We're ten billion miles from the sun," he pointed out. "Twenty degrees below zero? Are you kidding me? It gets colder than that in Canada!"

"Well let's be thankful," said Grandpa pragmatically, "that we're not in Canada. Now look. We'll park the ship and enter on foot. Our space suits will keep us fairly warm, but I don't know about the others...?"

As he said *others,* he turned to Wuztop and Headlice. Headlice just laughed and made a dismissive gesture with her hand.

"Twenty below is small change to me," she assured him. "I'm from Pluto, remember? I'll be fine out there. But I tell you what," she added fearfully—"I wouldn't want to take my chances in Canada!"

When they turned to Wuztop, he simply smirked.

"Watch," he said.

He removed his jacket and turned it deftly inside-out. Somehow, in the process, the garment was transformed from a thin jacket to a thick winter coat, complete with fur-lined hood.

Bradley was baffled.

"How did you do that?" he wondered.

"It's very versatile," said Wuztop simply.

Then they went through the bags from the Adventurers' Emporium. Bradley and Headlice hadn't bought everything on the list, simply because the arachnids had shown up before they could. Also, they hadn't been able to buy a laser rifle because they were only children. They *had* been able to buy laser swords from the place next door, possibly because the shopkeeper—a five-eyed octopoid from Neptune—couldn't guess their ages, any more than they could have guessed his.

Bradley had a go at one of the laser swords. Instead of a blade, it had a long thin rod with a hook at the end. On the end of the hook was a little round mirror with the shiny side pointing back towards the hilt.

"How does it work?" he wondered out loud.

When he squeezed the grip, there was a sound like a rocket screaming skyward. Suddenly, the space between hilt and mirror was filled with a shaft of hot red light. He could feel the heat of it through his glove as he swung the sword around, hearing it go *wom, wa-a-am, zrr-rr, ker-dink!*

"Careful with that," warned Grandpa—shoving the inflatable dinghy into his rucksack. "When it goes *ker-dink* it's about to overheat. Now take a rucksack. I'm not carrying everything by myself!"

Once they were ready, they climbed down the rope ladder and onto the surface of the strange planet. The cold air made Bradley's face numb. As he dropped down from the hatch, he felt like he was falling into icy water.

He took a couple of deep breaths. The air hurt his teeth a bit, but it was definitely breathable—just as Captain Nosegay had promised.

He was disappointed to see that the mountain with the mine entrance was quite a way off.

"Why have we landed here?" he wondered.

"The arachnids might be following," explained Grandpa simply. "If they find our spaceship next to an old abandoned mine, it won't take them long to put two and two together!"

"I suppose," said Bradley unhappily.

He felt something warm brush his neck and jumped. When he turned, it was just Waldo, with little beads of ice already forming on his whiskers.

"Oh!" said Bradley in surprise. "You're coming too, are you?"

The little star-pup dipped his whole body, seeming to nod in reply.

"Well make sure he doesn't wander off," warned Grandpa. "If he goes, he goes. We don't have time to hunt for a lost pet out here. Now let's get this show on the road!"

He led them in a brisk walk across the

glittering blue plain. The surface of the dwarf planet cracked and crunched underfoot. As they marched, the hole in the mountainside seemed to grow larger and larger.

They were soon climbing the icy foothills. After just a few minutes, Bradley was out of breath.

"Oh, stop huffing and puffing!" said Wuztop. "I could march all day when I was your age!"

"It's not my fault," complained Bradley unhappily. "My body isn't used to gravity any more. My legs must have got lazy. I'm normally much fitter than this," he added as an aside to Headlice.

"Oh, I'm sure," said Grandpa with a snort. "In fact, didn't I see you on World's Strongest Man once? Weren't you the big one with all the muscles?"

At last, they found themselves high on the mountainside. The dark mine gaped before them. Bradley didn't know if it was his imagination, or if the air coming out of it was slightly warm.

"Should I get the torches out?" he wondered.

Grandpa found his laser sword and switched it on.

"No need," he said simply.

He went on a little way ahead. As he made his way inside, the sword lit the icy walls around him. Icicles shone like ruby daggers.

"Come on," he told the rest.

Wuztop and Headlice followed, and moments later, Waldo zipped through the air to join them. Bradley scurried along at the rear, feeling awkward with his laser sword. He held it out before him, waving it nervously like a sparkler on Bonfire Night. He was in a paradoxical frame of mind where he was terrified that something might jump out at them, yet also keen to kill a monster with his sword and bask in glory. He reflected soberly on the fact that he couldn't have the glory without the danger, and wondered if there was a life lesson in that. Then he remembered that he was only a child anyway and quietly switched his laser sword off.

"Is it me," said Wuztop after a while, "or is it

getting warmer the further down we go?"

"It is," agreed Grandpa.

His sword went *wom, wa-a-am, zrr-rr!* as he shone it around.

"Much warmer. I wonder why?"

Bradley looked at Waldo. The ice beads on his fur were starting to melt. As Bradley watched, one turned to water and fell from the tip of a trembling white whisker.

"What kind of mine is this?" Bradley wondered out loud. "You never said."

"I don't actually know," admitted Grandpa. "The map seemed to call it a *fruit mine,* but I can't think what a fruit mine would be. I'm sure I just translated it badly."

As he spoke, they rounded a corner, and Bradley was surprised to see a little bright speck shining ahead of them.

"Daylight!" he cried.

Then it dawned on him that they were billions of miles from the sun. He scratched his head in puzzlement.

"Well it *looks* like daylight," he said at last.

"What is it?"

"No idea," admitted Grandpa. "Let's find out!"

He led them towards it. As they drew closer, there was no doubt at all that the air was getting warmer. Before long, it was positively humid. Bradley felt his forehead tingling, and was surprised to find droplets of sweat forming over his eyes.

"Wait! Stop!" cried Grandpa suddenly.

He spread his arms out, preventing the others from overtaking him.

"Listen," he said. "Can you hear that?"

Bradley held his breath and realised that he could. He could hear distant shrieking animals and whooping wildlife.

"It sounds like a zoo," he said. "What on earth is it?"

"Only one way to find out!" said Grandpa brightly. "Forward!"

At last, they spilled out into the open, blinking and covering their eyes. Bradley couldn't believe what he was seeing. Far below them, spreading out as far as the eye could see, was a thick green carpet of lush forest. The hot air buzzed with little flying creatures.

"Impossible!" said Wuztop—removing his thick winter coat. "Where in blue blazes are we?"

Bradley scanned the treetops below. Here and there, dark shapes flitted from branch to branch.

"Maybe we went through the portal," he suggested. "Maybe we got transported through space and time and just didn't notice?"

Grandpa didn't seem convinced. He looked down at the vibrant green jungle, then turned and squinted back into the tunnel. Then he straightened and pinched his moustache thoughtfully.

"Curious," he said at last.

"What?" wondered Bradley.

"I've got a theory," said Grandpa simply. "Hang on."

He reached into his bag and found an expensive pair of sunglasses. He put them on and turned his face skyward, staring at the sun.

"Ha ha!" he cried. "I *thought* so."

He passed the sunglasses around so they could all take a look. At last, it was Bradley's turn. When he put them on, he was able to stare directly at the sun, like Grandpa had done.

Except it wasn't a sun at all. It was an enormous flat slug, and its body gave off a fierce white light that filled the air for miles around.

Suddenly, Bradley realised that the sky wasn't real either. It was an enormous curved ceiling of light blue stone—the same stone, in fact, that the mountain had been made of—and the slug was splatted like a fried egg on the underside of it.

"We haven't gone anywhere," said Grandpa. "We're actually *inside* the dwarf planet, under the mountain—and that," he added, jerking a thumb skyward, "is a very rare creature called *Solortardus splendidus*—the magnificent sun-slug! It gives off enough light and heat to sustain a whole ecosystem, as you can plainly see. It also keeps the planet warm enough to walk on, even though it's so very far from the sun. We've essentially found a world within a world. Remarkable indeed."

Bradley watched as the magnificent sun-slug crawled very slowly up the rockface. It had frills and stripes like a sea-slug from Earth, and eight fiery eyes on waving stalks. The minute Bradley removed the sunglasses, it was lost in glare and he had to look away.

"Now that really is something," he said. "So what now?"

Grandpa got the map out and activated it. He inspected it from every angle and consulted his phrase book.

"Now we press on," he said. "The portal is hidden in the centre of the jungle—and for the record, I bet it's absolutely *teeming* with wildlife down there! What an adventure, eh?"

He stopped and scanned their blank faces.

"Well come on then!" he urged. "What are you waiting for? An invitation? Onward! Onward to the portal, and the gemstones of Pluto! Onward to glory!"

With a wild look on his face, he hurried them down the craggy rocks, taking them closer and closer to the dark jungle.

BANANAS AND PIRANHAS

THEY SPENT QUITE some time marching through trees, and Bradley soon got sick of it. Grandpa went on ahead, hacking at the undergrowth with his laser sword. Every now and then he stopped to consult the map, which was generally the sign for them to turn around and set off in an entirely different direction.

The jungle was like an Earth jungle, but subtly different in many ways. For instance, some of the trees had gigantic blue bananas growing in bunches, and suckered tentacles hanging like lianas.

"I guess it's a fruit mine after all," said Grandpa, looking up at the weird bananas. "I wonder what they taste like?"

There were little green monkeys swinging

from tree to tree. At least, they were *sort of* like monkeys. When one stopped long enough for Bradley to look at it, he saw that it had six arms, two tails, and an extra blinking eye in the middle of its forehead.

"Hello!" said Bradley.

"Hello yourself, Earthling," said the monkey—and off it went, swinging through the noisy canopy.

Further into the jungle, they found huge thorny bushes with hairy black berries.

"Children must *never* eat berries off bushes," said Grandpa sternly. "They might be poisonous. Luckily, I've got a gizmo that says if something is good to eat."

He felt in his rucksack and eventually found something that looked like a thermometer. When he touched it to one of the berries, the end lit up red.

"Good!" he said happily. "They're fine to eat."

He popped one in his mouth, chewed it, and was sick on the floor.

131

"My apologies," he said weakly. "Now I remember. The red light means it's *not* edible. Green means good to go."

A little later, they found a bush that had even bigger, lush-looking red ones. This time, the thermometer glowed green. Grandpa tried one and declared it delicious.

"Help me pick some!" he told the others.

They made two big piles, which Grandpa wrapped in paper. He twisted the corners and put the parcels in the top of Bradley's rucksack.

"We'll have those later," he promised.

And off they went through the jungle. After about an hour and a half, they stopped for a drink of water. As they passed the bottle around, Bradley spotted something overhead.

"Look!" he cried—pointing up through a gap in the canopy. "There!"

His heart sank. It was the arachnids' ship, shining like a venomous beetle. It crawled across the pretend blue sky, barely seeming to move at all.

"They must have followed us," said Grandpa.

"I guess their nippy little ship could fit through the tunnel. And now they're trying to find us."

Above the chattering wildlife, Bradley could just about hear the sound of the engines. The unwelcome spaceship hovered like a hawk, seeming to scan the treetops for prey.

"Let's press on," said Grandpa. "Or at the very least, get out of sight!"

They continued trekking through the jungle. Bradley began to wonder if he'd actually died and gone to some horrible kind of afterlife, where his punishment was to simply walk and walk forever—over icy plain, up a mountain, and through dense hot jungle—in a dreary, fruitless march without end.

Grandpa, however, was having the time of his life.

"I tell you what," he announced, swinging his laser sword this way and that—"you can't beat the feel of the sun on your face!"

Bradley scowled at him.

"You mean *slug* on your face," he said darkly. "That's what it is, Grandpa. A massive slug."

Grandpa was unperturbed.

"And you can't beat it," he finished happily. "Here. Let's have some of those berries."

Bradley passed him one of the paper parcels. The minute Grandpa opened it, the canopy exploded into life. A dozen little creatures dropped down from the trees and clung to his arms.

"Ambush!" cried Grandpa.

They looked like birds of paradise, but instead of wings they had grasping little hands. Clearly, they had their hearts set on the berries. When Grandpa tried to protect the fruit, they took fright and filled the air with bright green vapour. It seemed to come out of their armpits, and when Grandpa breathed it in, the effect was instantaneous.

"Ha ha!" he laughed drunkenly. "Here. Take 'em. Take 'em, you little rascals. Take the berries. I don't care. Why did we come here? I want to see a pantomime."

Then he sat down and refused to move. The little bird-things legged it into the undergrowth, taking as many berries as they could carry.

Before long, the effects of the green spray wore off. Grandpa was mortified, but soon rallied and led them deep into the jungle. The magnificent sun-slug crawled to the bottom of the dark stone sky and began to make a nest somewhere. The light faded to a soft, sleepy red and then vanished altogether.

They stopped and pitched the four man tent by torchlight. Then Grandpa turned the torch off to show them something.

"Look up," he told them—"through the treetops."

Bradley did, and was surprised to see what looked like stars.

"They're beautiful," said Headlice beside him. "What are they?"

"Why—baby sun-slugs, of course!" replied Grandpa. "Only one of them will become an adult. There isn't enough food to have two at once. Isn't nature wonderful?"

They made a fire and spit-roasted a giant blue banana over it. The gooey flesh was like banoffee trifle. Then, as the air cooled and the fire died, they got inside the tent, zipped it shut, and fell asleep on the lumpy ground sheet.

In the middle of the night, Bradley felt someone lightly rocking his shoulder.

"Bradley," whispered Headlice. "Bradley. Bradley. Bradley. Bradley."

He groaned and rubbed his eyes.

"Good grief. What?" he wondered.

"I couldn't sleep so I went outside," she told him. "I saw a shooting star!"

"But we're underground," he reminded her. "There *aren't* any stars. Just baby sun-slugs."

"Exactly!" she hissed. "So one of them must've fallen off!"

He felt a brief pang of pity for the poor baby sun-slug.

"Well there's nothing we can do about it," he said flatly.

"Well that's just the thing," she went on. "We *can* do something about it. It's very bright and I can see where it landed. But I don't want to get it by myself."

Bradley tried to ignore her. He had an opportunity to just close his eyes and be instantly asleep again. If he paid any more attention to her, he would soon be wide awake.

"Bradley?" she whispered. "Please?"

He sat up and glared at her in annoyance.

"All right," he said sternly. "Show me."

He saw the site of the impact straight away. Some distance away, through the dark shapes of the trees, was a wavering white light.

He turned on his laser sword, making red trees appear all around him. A strange creature with only one arm had been hanging from a branch. Startled by the light, it dropped to the ground and pulled itself clumsily into the undergrowth.

"Come on then," said Bradley.

They went through the jungle, hacking from time to time at tangled vegetation. As they neared the location of the strange light, it started to look like Headlice had been wrong.

"Oh," she said simply.

Standing in a little clearing, giving out a ghostly light, was an enormous white flower, with trembling petals that shone like silver. It bathed the whole clearing with artificial moonlight, making the trees and dripping plants seem even stranger and more magical. It was taller than a man, and fatter than a hippo, and the sight of it took Bradley's breath away.

"Blimey," he said.

He'd seen trees growing on asteroids, and pyramids on Mars, and meteors exploding in the sky over Grabelon, but the strange white flower was the most beautiful thing he had ever seen.

"Come on," he whispered to Headlice. "Let's go and investigate."

He climbed carefully out of the undergrowth, waving her to follow. They stood side by side before the enormous flower, watching the strange light shining through its petals.

"I thought it was the baby sun-slug," said Headlice. "I wonder what makes it shine?"

Then Bradley spotted something and smiled.

"Don't worry," he told her—"you were right all along. Look!"

He pointed to a white-hot blob inside one of the petals. As they watched, it crawled slowly down the inside of the flower.

"The slug landed right inside it," he explained. "That's why it's glowing. I wonder if we can get it out again?"

But before she could answer, they were interrupted.

"Have no fear, Earthling!" said a wise voice behind them. "The infant will be fine in the flower."

They jumped and turned. Hiding in the vegetation, bathed in the light from the baby sun-slug, was one of the green monkeys with the extra arms.

"Hello!" said Headlice. "But are you sure? Doesn't it belong high up on the rock?"

The monkey just smiled.

"It can feed on the flower's nectar," it assured her. "And so it should. High on the rock, it was just another infant, with almost no chance of becoming an adult. Here, at least, it will be a thing of beauty for as long as it lives."

With those words, the intelligent monkey sprang up into the air and grabbed the end of a long crooked branch.

"When the flower dies," it promised, "I will find it another. I and my children, and theirs after them. Farewell, Plutonian! Farewell, Earthling!"

And it swung off into the dark jungle, chattering as it went.

"Well at least we know the slug is safe," said Headlice—turning to watch its progress down the inside of the flower. "That's the main thing."

She followed it all the way down, losing herself in the sight of it. As Bradley watched, light and dark seemed to mix in the magical clearing, turning her face and hair to strange silver.

"We could come here once a week," she suddenly suggested—"to check on it!"

He looked around.

"What—here? To the dwarf planet? It's a bit of a trek," he reminded her bleakly.

As they stood there watching, he remembered how they'd first met, all those days ago in the Asteroid Belt. He remembered how scared he'd been by her reflection in the back of his spoon. Maybe he'd just got used to having her around, but suddenly, the fact that she was a one-eyed girl from Pluto no longer seemed especially odd or unsettling. In fact, out there—ten billion miles from the sun, in a slug-lit jungle deep beneath the foothills of an icy blue mountain—it was probably no odder, nor any more unsettling, than the fact that he was a two-eyed boy from planet Earth.

"It's a good job you woke me up," he told her. "I would have hated to miss this."

She smiled and gave him a playful punch.

"Right back at you," she said. "I would've slept through it if you hadn't been snoring!"

Then they climbed back into the undergrowth, and made their way in silence to the waiting tent.

* * *

The next morning, the magnificent slug returned to its station high on the rockface. They ate a hearty breakfast of roasted blue banana, watching the slug change colour overhead. During the course of their meal, it turned from deep volcanic red to dazzling white.

Once they'd eaten, they packed up the tent and went on their way. As they marched through the forest, Bradley kept looking over his shoulder. Everywhere they went, they seemed to be followed by the little bird-things that had ambushed them the day before. He watched them warily, remembering how they had stunned Grandpa with their green spray. Even when he couldn't see them, he could hear them squawking in the canopy above.

"Why are they following us?" he wondered. "I hope they don't spray us!"

"They can prob'ly smell the rest of the berries," replied Grandpa. "Don't unwrap them, whatever you do! You saw what happened last time, didn't you?"

Eventually, they found a wide rushing river that cut through the jungle.

"The portal to the treasure chamber," announced Grandpa, "is somewhere beyond this river."

"Well I can't swim," said Wuztop. "Not in *this* outfit. It's dry clean only. Did we remember to bring a dinghy?"

Bradley thought back to the Adventurers' Emporium.

"Yes," he said at last. "Well we certainly bought one. And I think I saw Grandpa put it in his rucksack."

Grandpa tutted, unshouldered his bag, and began to empty it. He pulled out a torch, some cheap-looking flip-flips, a big bag of crisps, a comical pair of long johns, a chain of brightly-coloured hankies all tied together, and a bouquet of garish paper flowers, sniggering as he did.

"That's not funny," Bradley told him. "You're not a magician. Get on with it."

"All right, all right," muttered Grandpa—tossing the flowers into the river. "Hang on. It's in here somewhere."

At last, he found the dinghy. When he unrolled it on the grass like a big floppy tongue, Bradley saw that it had a plastic contraption attached to the back of it, with a big red button just waiting to be pushed.

Grandpa toed it lightly, then stomped on it with relish.

The contraption began to make a warm rushing sound like a hair dryer. Straight away, the rest of the dinghy started to swell unevenly. Now it looked like a tongue that had been stung by bees.

That much, Bradley had expected. It was, after all, a self-inflating dinghy.

But when it rose weightlessly into the air and began to flash all over like a pinball machine, he was quite surprised.

"Why's it doing that?" he wondered.

"To keep itself dry," explained Grandpa. "Why? What did you expect? It's not one of

144

your boring old *Earth* dinghies, Bradley. This is a space dinghy! If all goes to plan, we won't actually make contact with the water."

"And a good job too," said Wuztop fearfully. "Look!"

He was pointing to the bouquet of flowers that had been thrown into the water. They were still in view because they'd caught on a rock instead of rushing downstream. Now they were jerking around in a strange way, as if something had started tugging them under the surface.

Suddenly, the paper flowers were torn apart. A flurry of bright confetti flew up into the air, then landed on the water and rushed away.

"Piranhas," said Wuztop darkly. "Don't fall overboard, whatever you do!"

Bradley and Headlice shared an unhappy look as they got in the front. Waldo floated to join them, then settled on a spot by Bradley's knees.

Just as Wuztop was climbing awkwardly into the back, they were ambushed.

"Halt!" roared a voice.

The arachnid assassins came screeching down

145

from the sky, riding machines that looked like giant wasps.

"Stop right there!" cried the largest of them. "The fun ends here!"

Five of his eyes were hidden by patches, but the other three shone with a wicked light. As he rode down from the sky, he held a gun high above his head. It went *pee-ow, pee-ow!* as he fired off a couple of warning shots.

"I'm the Black Baron!" he bellowed. "The most feared assassin in the Solar System! And if you value your lives more than treasure," he warned them with relish, "you'll give us the map and turn back here. Hand it over, or I'll shoot you in a heartbeat."

Grandpa looked at him in disgust.

"You'd kill us for treasure?" he said with contempt. "What kind of monster are you?"

The Baron just shrugged.

"I've killed better men for less," he replied.

Then something occurred to him, and he smiled a nasty smile.

"So do you want to know how I found you,"

he offered, "in all this dense dark jungle?"

Grandpa shrugged.

"Sure," he said. "Surprise me."

The Baron smirked.

"I pulled one of those little glowing slugs off the rockface," he said, "and tossed it into the forest. It was just a matter of time before the children came to investigate. Then we trailed them back to your tent."

Headlice gasped.

"Oh no! It was *my* fault they found us!" she whispered to Bradley.

He shook his head.

"Don't worry," he assured her kindly. "It was totally worth it. And I bet they would have found us anyway."

The Baron grinned at the touching scene.

"So do I," he agreed. "Oh, and by the way— before your little *Plutonian* friend tries to crash our flying machines, I ought to warn you that it won't work. We resprayed 'em all with lead paint. They're totally impervious to her brain waves."

Bradley groaned.

"Good grief," he said. "Not *that* again. It's not true! It's just a nasty little story!"

The Baron just shrugged.

"Better safe than sorry," he pointed out. "Now one of you, quick—cough up the map!"

Grandpa stroked his moustache and seemed to think it over. Then he grinned and jumped in the back of the dinghy, almost throwing Bradley from the front.

"Full speed ahead!" cried the intrepid old astronaut. "Off we go, to find the gemstones of Pluto!"

The dinghy must have been voice-operated. It shot off like a rocket, raising up a curtain of cold water, and poor Waldo had to go flying through the spray. The arachnids howled with frustration and gave chase on their giant wasps, zigging and zagging over the water.

Bradley looked over his shoulder. The Baron was sighting them down his pistol.

"Grandpa!" he warned. "We're going to get shot!"

"Nonsense!" Grandpa assured him. "Dinghy! Starboard!"

The weightless rubber boat veered sharply to the right. So sharply, in fact, that Bradley came face-to-face with the surface of the water, and saw the hungry little fish that were squirming underneath it.

"Dinghy! Port!" barked Grandpa.

It banked the other way, just in time for them to dodge a volley of gunfire. Where the energy bolts struck the water, steam rose into the air.

Then a rucksack went overboard. It was gobbled in a flash by hungry little jaws. Bradley grabbed Headlice to stop her joining it.

"You can't escape!" roared the Baron behind them—letting off another volley. "Stop now and give me the map!"

Wuztop made a noise of frustration, then reached into a bag and pulled something out of it.

"I've had enough of this," he muttered. "It's not worth it. Here! Take the map!" he cried—throwing it behind him.

As it flew through the air, it split into pages that fluttered and flapped.

"Don't let them land in the water!" shrieked the Baron to his followers—screeching to a halt mid-air. "Catch them! Catch them quick! Don't let the piranhas get them!"

Soon, the arachnids were far behind, desperately trying to catch and reassemble the loose pages. Grandpa looked over his shoulder and frowned.

"Pages?" he wondered. "The map didn't have *pages*, Wuztop. Blistering black holes! What did you throw?"

The tailor wrung his hands and grinned awkwardly.

"Your novel?" he suggested nervously.

"My *novel?*" bellowed Grandpa. "Why—you rascal!—you little—ooh!"

He turned a dangerous shade of red, then quickly composed himself.

"We'll worry about that later," he decided with a growl. "For now, we've got treasure to find. Onward!"

PERIL AT THE PORTAL

ON THE OTHER side of the river, they found an ancient stone temple buried in lush vegetation. Brightly-coloured lemurs perched on the roof, looking suspiciously down at the intruders.

Grandpa consulted the map. In the glare of the jungle, the three-dimensional image was barely visible.

"Blimey," he said suddenly. "We're here. The portal's right inside!"

Wuztop rolled his eyes.

"Well thank goodness!" he said. "What are we waiting for?"

He hurried them towards the door,

"Come on!" he insisted. "I've had enough of this jungle. I want to find the treasure and get that reward!"

The interior was dark and cool, with thin rays of light cutting through tiny slit windows. The portal itself was a big round hole in the wall opposite, and Bradley saw that it was swimming with a kind of strange blue plasma. An enormous metal statue stood solemnly over it, one leg on either side. As they stood around staring, about half a dozen bird-things gathered by the entrance, peering hungrily into the temple.

Bradley ignored them and looked up at the statue's face. It had little blank eyes and big lips, and enormous ears made of beaten metal.

Suddenly, he realised who it looked like. Other than the fact that it was twenty feet tall instead of tiny, and metallic grey instead of green, it resembled the annoying little man who had given them the map.

"It looks like Benzo!" said Bradley out loud. "Blimey. It feels like *ages* since we last saw him. I wonder what happened to him?"

Grandpa was inspecting the portal.

"Hmm? What? Benzo? Well I hope he's

dead," he said bitterly. "I hope he jumped off a cliff."

Bradley was horrified.

"Grandpa!" he gasped. "That's a *terrible* thing to say!"

"It's actually not," said Grandpa. "That's the way it is. Haven't I told you how it works on Mercury? There's no such thing as *old age* there. They don't grow old and die like we do. But their brains wither over time, and when they start to lose their marbles, they just call it a day and jump off a cliff. I mean, don't get me wrong—they're all a *bit* loopy. But they get worse and worse, and if they don't jump, it's just a matter of time before they get pushed. It all sounds horrible, but on Mercury, it's just the way it is."

Bradley digested that.

"I see," he said. "So is Benzo very old then?"

Grandpa let out a short, humourless laugh.

"He must be!" he muttered. "He's well past his sell-by date. Pretty sure he knows it, too. He's running from his fate. Can't say I blame him. No one wants to die, do they?"

He leaned forward to stare at the portal. Cold blue flames licked the air in front of him.

"It's not nice," he admitted. "But remember you're in space. It can't *all* be star-pups and fizzy pop. Now are we going through this portal, or do we hang around and let the arachnids catch us?"

"I'm afraid the answer," snarled a voice behind them, "is the latter."

Bradley froze.

"Turn around slowly," said the voice, "and don't make any sudden movements."

The Black Baron did *not* look happy. He was soaking wet from head to toe and covered in little red scratches, but he had his pistol held out towards them, and the wicked light still burned in his eyes.

"No one loses me for long," he said darkly. "A portal, eh? Does it lead to the treasure?"

He gestured for Grandpa to step away from it. Moments later, his cronies entered the temple behind him, looking equally dishevelled.

154

"Imagine my dismay," began the Baron coldly, "when I stopped to inspect my so-called map. I spent half an hour getting those pages together. Half an hour. Just picture me, up to my elbows in piranha-infested water, for half an hour. And what's my reward? Nothing. Nothing whatsoever. Just the turgid prose," he finished bitterly, "of a man who thinks that *collectible* has an 'a' in it."

Grandpa looked shocked, then cackled with triumph.

"Aha!" he cried. "It *does* have an 'a' in it! Egg on *your* face, Baron!"

Before the Baron could reply, something very strange happened. The whole temple began to shake. Sand-coloured masonry fell from the ceiling, hitting the ground and shattering.

"Sweet rings of Saturn!" swore Grandpa, jumping out of the way. "What's going on?"

The metal statue opened its mouth and roared a terrible, artificial roar. As Bradley watched in horror, it wrenched one arm free of the wall, then the other, then flexed all ten of its enormous metal fingers. Finally, it uprooted its feet and shook moist dark earth from between its toes.

"Intruders!" it bellowed. *"Intruders! Engage kill mode!"*

The smaller arachnids took one look and ran away. The furious Baron stood his ground, lining up a shot with his pistol.

"Come back, cowards! Where are you going? It's only a robot! Watch!"

To prove his point, he fired off a volley of shots. They didn't stop the monster. They just scorched the surface of the metal, leaving dirty little marks all over its belly.

"Intruders!" insisted the giant robot. It squatted like a Sumo wrestler, blocking the way to the portal. *"Kill mode engaged! Commence kill mode!"*

Bradley looked around in desperation. The temple had a stone pillar in each corner. One was overgrown with some kind of insistent creeping ivy, so dense that it made a kind of den.

"Grandpa!" he said. "Look!"

The old man followed his trembling finger, then nodded quickly.

"Good thinking," he agreed. "Come on, all of you!"

Waldo didn't need telling twice. He zipped through the air and hid himself high in the den. As the rest ran to join him, he peeped out from the dense green foliage, regarding the rampaging robot with horror.

Grandpa pushed Bradley and Headlice into the vegetation, then jumped in and waved for Wuztop to follow. There was plenty of room behind the curtain of tangled woody stems. They sat huddled in the darkness with their backs to the pillar, smelling the rich, earthy smell of the ivy, then listened in horror as the angry robot pulverised the temple.

Once Grandpa got his breath back, he whistled in disbelief.

"By the Great Red Spot!" he swore. "Must be some kind of guardian, left to guard the treasure!"

157

Then his eyes lit up and he grinned in the gloom.

"Which means it must be worth a fortune!" he said with relish.

Suddenly, a pair of strong, purple hands wrenched the ivy apart. The Baron looked at them in disgust.

"Look at you—hiding in a bush like little hedgehogs!" he sneered. "Where's your fighting spirit, eh?"

Grandpa rolled his eyes, then grabbed the Baron and pulled him close.

"Listen," he hissed. "There's only one way we're going to make it out of this alive. We need to work together!"

The Baron looked surprised, then got hold of Grandpa and hauled him out from behind the pillar.

"Well as long as you're prepared to be the *bait*," he smirked, "I'm sure we'll work together just fine!"

In a heartbeat, Wuztop sprang to Grandpa's aid. He activated his laser sword and pounced, swinging it overhead. It sliced through the hanging ivy, singed poor Waldo's fur, and swung down towards the Baron's shoulder.

The Baron, however, was too quick for Wuztop.

He didn't even let go of Grandpa. He just stepped out of reach, then lunged back in to deliver a crushing karate chop, right on Wuztop's wrist.

Wuztop had been swinging the sword back up again. He released it in shock and watched it fly into the air. Before it even had chance to come back down, the Baron struck him once on the chin, knocking him out cold.

"Come on!" said Bradley to Headlice. "Move!"

He yanked her out of the way as Wuztop fell to earth, followed shortly by the fiery spinning sword. Then the Baron left, dragging Grandpa to meet his fate.

Moments later, Bradley jumped to his feet in a panic.

"Stay there!" he told Headlice.

He poked his head out from behind the pillar.

The Baron had taken Grandpa to the far side of the temple and had him in a crushing headlock.

"Come on!" he roared to the rampaging robot. "You want to kill the intruders, don't you? Well here we are! Come away from that blasted portal!"

The robot began to stomp slowly towards them. Suddenly, Bradley saw what the Baron had planned. He was going to tempt the robot over, then drop Grandpa and run to the portal. He was banking on Grandpa to keep the robot occupied while he made a dash for the treasure.

Bradley's heart sank. He didn't know what to do.

Through the far-off entrance, he could see that the sun-slug was setting, changing colour as it crawled down the sky.

He could see that brightly-coloured lemurs were dropping to the ground and fleeing the temple as it shook under them.

He could see the river too. The water sparkled like red cellophane, reflecting a ruby light that made the scene in the temple look positively infernal.

At last—just as he was starting to despair—he felt someone tugging his arm.

"Bradley," said Headlice urgently. "Let me past. I can deal with this."

He looked at her in disbelief.

"What do you mean, deal with it? How?"

"Honestly. I know what to do. But I don't want you to watch me doing it," she said sadly.

He looked at the robot, then shook his head.

"No way," he said. "You need to stay here."

He tried to push her deeper into the ivy, but she fought back and grabbed both of his wrists.

"Listen! Bradley! You've *got* to trust me. I'm the only one here who can fix this!"

When he didn't reply, she groaned in annoyance and just shoved him out of the way. He stepped sideways, trying to keep his balance, but got his feet tangled in the ivy.

There was nothing he could do. He sat heavily on his backside, then watched in horror as she strode out into the centre of the temple.

"Headlice!" he shouted.

His heart began to pound.

Grandpa was trapped in the Baron's tight grip and the robot was stomping towards them. In a second, it would reach them.

In the meantime, Wuztop was out cold, *he* was stuck in ivy, and Headlice was marching to her doom.

Then something extraordinary happened.

She stopped behind the robot, lowered her head, and pressed her fingers to her temples. As she rubbed them, the air began to crackle and glow around her.

The robot stopped awkwardly, as if it had forgotten what it was meant to be doing. A moment later, it took a single heavy step and then stopped again.

The Baron was astonished.

"Well, well, well!" he said at last—watching her press her temples as the robot struggled. "It *is* true! Your brains *do* mess with electronics!"

The robot, meanwhile, was trying to mobilise itself. Sparks began to crackle at the base of its neck and all around its shoulders.

Then it grunted, shook its head to clear it, and turned to face its tormentor.

"Headlice! Come back!" cried Bradley—trying to free his foot from the ivy. "It hasn't worked!"

He looked around desperately, hoping to spot something useful. He was surprised to see half a dozen bird-things hopping towards him, looking hopefully at his backpack. Apparently, they hadn't noticed the giant robot smashing up the temple and still had their hearts set on berries.

He groaned. The last thing he needed was for one to take fright and spray him in the face.

Then his eyes lit up.

He had an idea.

Being careful not to startle them, he unzipped his bag and took out the wrapped berries. The bird-things paid attention but hung back nervously, following the parcel with their hungry eyes.

"Not yet!" he told them.

In the meantime, Headlice had redoubled her efforts. The light around her grew even brighter. The robot roared with anger, then raised a giant metal leg to stomp her underfoot.

The enormous metal toes curled right over her.

"*Kill intruder!*" cried the metal monster. "*Kill intruder!*"

But as it roared, Headlice roared back, and the light around her intensified to a hot white glare.

The robot stood there on one leg, wobbling as sparks shot out of its enormous ears.

And then... it locked up entirely.

At last—like a tree going over in a forest—it began to topple.

And then it hit the floor, making the sandy tiles explode into dust.

The Baron ignored it. His three good eyes were fixed on the portal.

"So long, suckers!" he cried—making a sudden dash for it. "I'm outta here!"

But Bradley was ready to execute his plan. He threw the paper parcel with all his might. As it tumbled through the air, it began to unravel, shedding lush red berries all over the floor.

The little bird-things squawked with delight. Just as Bradley had hoped, they gave chase, holding out their little claws.

The Baron's eyes widened, but he didn't have time to duck. He collided face-first with the parcel, making it burst in a shower of juice and pulp. The berries landed in the creases of his clothes. He tried to wipe them from his eyes and body, but the bird-things shot up his legs and made for the fruit.

"Get away from me!" he roared—trying to fight them off.

His attackers looked startled, then raised their little arms in unison.

Soon, the Baron was surrounded by heady green vapour.

"What are you doing?" he wondered—breathing it in. "Get off me!"

And then he smiled a stupid smile.

"Heh heh!" he said. "Listen to me. *Get off me. Get off me.* I'm so strict!"

Before long, he was sitting on the floor, laughing to himself as he fed the berries to his new friends. Then he lay on his back and went to sleep, smiling through his mandibles.

Bradley couldn't believe his luck. He watched the Baron for a while to check he was asleep, then grinned at Headlice.

"We did it!" he told her.

At last, he managed to pull his foot free from the ivy. That done, he went to inspect Wuztop, who was groaning softly and looking around with one eye open.

"Come on," he told him gently. "Let's get you out of there!"

He helped the groggy blue tailor to his feet. Not long after, Grandpa sprang out from behind the toppled robot.

"I'm alive!" he announced brightly. "Excellent work, Headlice! Fancy that. Plutonian brains really *can* fry the electronics! Well, don't worry.

Your secret is safe with me."

She looked surprised.

"What—so it doesn't bother you? I mean, I *could* crash the spaceship after all," she reminded him. "Just like everyone says."

Grandpa jerked a thumb towards Bradley.

"So could he," he pointed out. "All he'd have to do is grab a lever or stick a bag on my head. But he'd never dream of it," he reminded her, "and neither would you. You've proved today that you're a dependable member of this crew, and I would trust you to the ends of the universe. You too, Bradley. That was quite a trick with the berries."

After a while, Bradley, Wuztop, and Waldo emerged from their corner of the temple. Wuztop looked slightly wobbly but managed a weak smile. All five of them gathered by the fallen robot and turned to the portal.

"Well this is it," said Grandpa—almost sounding sad. "The adventure's at an end. All that remains is to collect the treasure."

He looked down at the Baron, who was

snoring happily on the floor.

"We better leave before he wakes up," he pointed out. "Come on!"

THE GEMSTONES OF PLUTO

THE SHINING BLUE portal whisked them away in a heartbeat. When Bradley opened his eyes, he saw that they had come to a small gloomy room. It certainly didn't *look* like a treasure chamber. It was full of old wooden crates and boxes of bric-à-brac. The door had been bricked up many years before, leaving just a few narrow cracks, and the only exit was another blue portal.

Next to that, Bradley could see a sort of glass-fronted cabinet, full of cogs that went round and round in near-silence. They were all different colours—silver and gold and clean pink copper—and here and there, a strange light shone behind them, making them gleam in a weird way.

Grandpa was pointing his torch at every inch of the dirty wet walls.

"Where's the treasure?" he wondered bleakly. "The gemstones of Pluto? They've *got* to be here! Don't tell me we have to go through all these boxes..."

He went to the cabinet and bent to inspect it. The inner workings barely made any sound at all. There was a little brass plaque screwed to the front, and when Grandpa read it with the torch, he gasped in surprise.

"Good grief!" he said. "You're not going to believe this but—the portal brought us back to Grabelon! Right under my home town! This is the long-lost machine that summons the meteors. Remember?"

Bradley nodded. They had arrived there by bubble, watching the meteors flare and pop in the dark sky. The memory made the hairs rise on the back of his neck.

"It hasn't been seen for *centuries*," added Grandpa. "Some Mercurials must have hidden the treasure here when they were helping to build the city. Maybe the gems are hidden inside it...?"

Wuztop, meanwhile, had found something on the other side of the room. It was about the size of a microwave oven and had been left on a little wooden table.

"What's this?" he wondered—shining his own torch down at it.

Bradley went to look. He stepped carefully over a box full of crockery and glassware, then snorted when he saw what it was.

"It's just an ice dispenser," he told him. "Looks like it's plugged in. I wonder if it still works...?"

He reached down to the box at his feet, selected a dusty glass tumbler, and held it under the machine. To his surprise, it made a loud rattling noise and spat out enormous chunks of wet ice. He held up the glass and watched them glinting in the torchlight.

"Huh. Still works," he observed.

He turned the glass this way and that, watching droplets condense on the outside of it.

"Fancy that," he muttered.

Then he saw a old sticker on the ice machine and wiped the dust off. When he read it, his heart sank. The sticker said *Pluto Gem®* in shiny foil letters, with *Pluto Gemini Ice Machines, Inc.* in tiny black print below.

"Grandpa?" he said nervously. "You're not going to like this but—I think I've found the gemstones of Pluto!"

Grandpa span on the spot. Bradley held up the ice for him to see.

"Look," he said. "You told me once that Pluto was full of ice. Well, think about it. I think the gemstones of Pluto are just ice cubes."

Grandpa looked horrified, then shook his head.

"The gemstones of Pluto," he reminded him firmly, "are clearer and brighter than stars—with glittering facets that catch the light!"

"Well yeah," said Bradley—holding up the tumbler. "Look at them!"

Grandpa scanned the room frantically.

"But there's a magic goblet," he reminded

him. "A magic goblet, that refills itself when you pour them out! The king used to hand out whole cups of them on feast days! Where's the magic goblet?"

"Grandpa—this *is* the magic goblet," said Bradley. "Watch."

He shook the ice cubes onto the floor, then held the tumbler under the dispenser. The machine rumbled and refilled it with fresh ice.

"See?" he told Grandpa—giving the glass a light shake. "*That's* your magic goblet. I'm not being funny, but there's nothing special about free cups of ice. They do that at Nando's."

Grandpa had gone quite pale.

"But the map said they were rarer than diamonds!" he said desperately. "How is *ice* rarer than diamonds?"

Wuztop laughed humourlessly.

"I'm sure on Mercury," he reminded them, "ice really *is* rarer than diamonds. Think how hot it is!"

Grandpa had nothing to say to that. At last, his face fell.

173

"Sweet rings of Saturn! You're right. How disappointing! Still," he said philosophically, "it's no good crying over spilt milk. And at least I got to see the long-lost meteor machine, eh? To an old man from the City of Meteors, that's something quite special! Now let's get this treasure to the king."

He tucked the torch under his arm, went to the ice maker, and unplugged it from the wall. Then he lifted it off the table and carried it towards the portal.

"Come on!" he said brightly. "Let's see what's happening on Mercury!"

The king's throne room was a vast expanse of cool white marble, enclosed in a coffee-coloured bubble on the loftiest peak of the Mountains of Heat. When they materialised right in the middle of it, the armed guards jumped with surprise, then ran to circle them with guns raised.

"Wait! Stop!" roared the little king—waving them aside. "Is that—is that what I think it is?"

His throne was a huge column of glittering gold. It was crooked and crystalline, with a cushion for him to sit on, and he almost fell off the top of it in surprise.

"I don't believe it!" he said incredulously— straightening his crown. "He did it! Benzo *did* it!"

Grandpa cleared his throat.

"Tell us, Your Highness—who exactly *is* Benzo?"

The king shrugged.

"Just some guy," he said. "But it was his lifelong quest to find the treasure. He bought the map when he was very young. Then he lost it—hundreds and hundreds of years ago—and said he wouldn't rest until he got it back."

Grandpa's eyes widened.

"*Hundreds* of years?" he repeated. "Blimey. He really *was* old, wasn't he?"

"Ha!" cried the king. "Wasn't he just! We haven't seen him here for years, thank heaven. When he hears that the treasure is back, maybe he'll do the decent thing and finally jump off that cliff."

Grandpa beamed serenely.

"And that," he assured the king with a deep bow, "will mean more to me than all the treasure in the universe."

The king nodded graciously. Then he laughed and clapped his hands, and called for the guards to plug the ice maker in.

The view from the throne room was quite something. Through the darkened glass, the sun was clearly visible: a searing white disc, hot and huge, making the foothills glow like embers below. Mercury itself was made of scorched barren rock, stretching as far as the eye could see.

But it wasn't deserted. Here and there, lumbering horned creatures paced from crater to crater, grazing at the rock. They had eight legs apiece, Bradley saw, and must have been bigger than the biggest dinosaur.

They didn't just graze. From time to time, two of them would lock horns. Bradley watched from above, fascinated by their antics, while the king and his men celebrated behind him.

After a while, someone passed him a nice cool glass of fizzy pop.

"Hello Bradley," said Headlice. "How do you feel?"

"Ha ha. Tired," he replied without turning. "Thanks."

He took a swig of the drink, enjoying the dull glassy sound of the jostling ice. Then he wiped his cold wet lips.

"Has Grandpa asked about the reward?" he asked her.

She laughed.

"The king offered him fifty quid for it," she told him. "He's taking it well, but Wuztop is livid. It won't cover that new spaceship he wanted."

The minute she said *spaceship*, something occurred to Bradley, and his eyes widened.

"Spaceship!" he repeated. "Good grief! How will we get out of here? How will I get home? It's at the other end of the Solar System!"

She just waved dismissively.

"Oh, don't worry—I asked about that," she assured him. "Grandpa says that Captain Nosegay isn't stupid, and when he gets tired of waiting he'll just bring the ship and meet us here. But we *are* stuck until he picks us up."

She poked at her drink with a plastic straw.

"So when are you going back home?" she wondered shyly.

His face fell.

"What, to Earth? Well I don't know," he admitted. "They all know where I am 'cos I left a note, but I can't stay in space forever. If nothing else, I've missed loads of school. Did I tell you about my mum?"

She nodded.

"Well I should really sort that out," he said. "I still haven't brought it up with Grandpa."

She shrugged.

"Well you have to do what you think's best," she said. "And you can think it over while we wait for the spaceship."

He didn't have much else to say, and before

long she waved sweetly and wandered off with her drink.

"You should come and join the party," she said over her shoulder. "It's fun!"

A little while later he turned to see what was happening. Hundreds of little green men had flooded the throne room. The king himself had come down from his throne to serve iced drinks. His minstrel had produced a tiny little keyboard with a Bossa Nova setting, and was now improvising a slightly South American-sounding song about their adventures.

Grandpa was delighted by the attention. After a while they got him to perch on a tiny chair and tried to hoist him skyward, like the groom at a Jewish wedding. Sadly, they were too small to do anything other than jerk the chair forwards by about an inch, which was applauded by all as a huge triumph.

Bradley smiled.

Then a weightless shape emerged from the crowd and came floating towards him. It was

Waldo coming to join him. He stroked the star-pup's fur and turned back to the view, taking in the smouldering foothills, the barren rocky plains, the huge slow beasts with their big blunt horns, and the enormous white sun like a hole in the sky.

It was strange to see the sun seem so utterly alien. Not long ago, he'd seen it shrunk to the size of the coldest, smallest star. Now it was there among the mountains of Mercury, three times its normal size, and so close that he needed protective glass to stop it setting his hair on fire.

That was space though. Always something different. Always something strange.

Maybe he wouldn't go home *just* yet, he decided.

There was always tomorrow, or the next day— or the day after that.

And he smiled at the thought, then went to find Headlice.

To be continued...

Stay tuned to hear where our heroes go next! What lies in store for this intrepid crew? The oceans of Neptune? The methane mines of Makemake? The ice-filled craters of Callisto?!

Only one way to find out! Stick around, dear reader, and eagerly await...

The next gripping sequel to...

The Astronaut's Apprentice!

ALSO AVAILABLE FROM FALCON BERGER BOOKS...

THE ASTRONAUT'S APPRENTICE

BY PHILIP THREADNEEDLE

Bradley is a normal boy who lives on a farm. One night, his long lost alien Grandpa sneaks home in a flying saucer. They embark on a whirlwind tour of Outer Space, armed with nothing but their wits, some seriously stylish space suits, and a bottle of Gee Whiz Soda. Along the way, they meet a tailor from the Asteroid Belt, a one-eyed girl from Pluto, and an exploding alien called Waldo.

Don't miss your chance to meet Grandpa—the original space-aged pensioner!

Available from major online bookstores.

The TRUMBLE-BUGGINS
BY HARRY LADD

"OLLY AND CYNTHIA Trumblebuggins were the worst children you could ever hope to meet. You might think that you have some horrible children at your school, but in every way you can think of, and in every way that you can't, Olly and Cynthia were worse."

Naughty children are seldom popular, and between them, the Trumblebuggins children have Crackpot Juniors screaming for mercy. When they are finally expelled, their father must figure out a plan to get them back to school or else face his wife's fury. He quickly enlists the help of his drinking buddy, Mr Catchratter: a dubious genius, whose convoluted schemes leave lots to be desired...

Available from major online bookstores.

Printed in Great Britain
by Amazon.co.uk, Ltd.,
Marston Gate.